one thousand hills

JAMES ROY + NOËL ZIHABAMWE

one

thousand

hills

Scholastic Canada Ltd.
Toronto New York London Auckland Sydney
Mexico City New Delhi Hong Kong Buenos Aires

Scholastic Canada Ltd.
604 King Street West, Toronto, Ontario M5V 1E1, Canada

Scholastic Inc.
557 Broadway, New York, NY 10012, USA

Scholastic Australia Pty Limited
PO Box 579, Gosford, NSW 2250, Australia

Scholastic New Zealand Limited
Private Bag 94407, Botany, Manukau 2163, New Zealand

Scholastic Children's Books
Euston House, 24 Eversholt Street, London NW1 1DB, UK

www.scholastic.ca

Library and Archives Canada Cataloguing in Publication

Roy, James, 1968-, author
One thousand hills / James Roy and Noël Zihabamwe.

Previously published: Parkside SA: Omnibus Books, 2016.
Issued in print and electronic formats.
ISBN 978-1-4431-5760-5 (paperback).--ISBN 978-1-4431-5761-2 (html)

I. Zihabamwe, Noël, author II. Title.

PZ7.R81215On 2017   j823'.914   C2016-905308-3
                                              C2016-905309-1

Originally published by Scholastic Australia, 2016.
This edition published by Scholastic Canada Ltd. in 2017.
Typeset in 11.5/16.5pt Caslon by Heidi Goeldi.
Text copyright © 2016 by James Roy & Noël Zihabamwe.
Cover design copyright © 2016 by Steve Wells.
Photos © Shutterstock, Inc.: cover background (naturemania), cover grunge texture (ilolab
and Nejron Photo), cover and iii boy (Chalermsak), cover and iii grass (Dario Sabljak), cover
and iii hill (Maxim Ibragimov).
All rights reserved.

6 5 4 3 2 1   Printed in Canada 139   17 18 19 20 21

This book is dedicated to every child hiding or running in fear because of conflicts that have nothing to do with them — JR

In memory of my late parents, Emmanuel and Judith Zihabamwe, who gave me so much, which has enabled me to give back to the global community — NZ

Are you comfortable there?

I'm fine, I guess. What happens now?

You start talking. Do you need a glass of water before we begin?

What do I talk about?

That all depends. What do you *want* to talk about?

Nothing. I don't want to talk about anything. I told Monsieur Baume that already.

Okay.

Okay?

Okay.

So I don't have to talk if I don't want to?

That's right.

So will we just sit here until recess? If I don't say anything, I mean.

Yes, Pascal, if that's what you want to do.

And then I'll go to recess and you'll go back to the staff room?

Yes, something like that.

Will you still get paid? Even if I don't tell you anything, do you still get paid?

Yes, of course. Don't worry about me.

But I don't want you to get in trouble.

That's very kind of you, Pascal, but it's fine, honestly. Who would I get in trouble with, anyway?

Monsieur Baume?

I don't have to worry about being called to the principal's office.

That's lucky for you.

No, I did all that when *I* was in secondary school. I went to a Catholic school too, you know. But not this one. It was in France, actually.

Did you get in trouble a lot?

Not a lot. A bit. Enough.

What sort of thing did you do?

Oh, you know. The usual ...

Did you ever smash another boy's head into a locker?

No. No, I don't think I ever did that. But I remember that sometimes I felt like it.

Sure you did.

I did. Sometimes.

Well, I feel like it a *lot*. But this is the first time I did it. True.

Do you want to talk about that?

About how I feel? Not really.

Okay.

Are you even a real priest?

Me? No. I'm not a priest at all. I'm just a counsellor.

So you're not a priest.

No. As I said, I'm a counsellor. Well, a child psychologist, actually, but —

I'm not crazy.

I know you're not crazy, Pascal. Why would you think —

You said that you're a psychologist.

Yes, that's right. You might be thinking of something different. Anyway, just think of me as someone to listen to you, that's all. *If* you talk, that is. Which you don't have to do.

Okay.

But I'll be honest — I am interested in something you said just a minute ago. Or rather, the way you said it. When you asked if I was a priest, and I said I wasn't, you seemed relieved.

I don't care if you're a priest.

You don't?

No. Back in Agabande I had friends who were priests.

What were their names?

Father Oscar was my best priest friend.

Were there others?

Sure, but he was my favourite one. He used to talk to me a lot. His hand was all bent and twisted, like this . . . For a while, I thought about going to the seminary, just because of him. Because I wanted to be like him.

Do you still think about that? About going into the priesthood?

No, not any more.

Can you tell me why not?

Because of Father Michel.

Don't you mean Father Oscar?

No, I meant Father Michel.

I don't understand.

4

It's a long story.

I've got plenty of time. I've got all the time in the world.

Agabande, Musanze District, Northern Rwanda

This story starts with a bell.

There's also the slanting sun, and the hawks overhead. The rooster and the goat and the town and the mist and the church above the clouds. There's the radio, with its message that chilled the boy to the bone. The night in the broken water tank when the chickens were panicking outside, and the water tasted like stale beer. Don't forget the mother and the father and the brother and the boy who was more like a brother, and the sister. Baby, too. Please don't forget Baby. Or the man who was an enemy before he was a friend, even just for a little while.

And there was the dying.

Of course there's the dying. For many, that's all this was ever about. It's all it will ever be about, until they can let it go. Which is hard. Very hard. Almost the hardest thing of all.

But the bell. Mostly the bell. For this child, the bell was everything. The beginning of it all and, in a way, the end of it all.

At the beginning, in a sense, it heralded his first memory.

Pascal's first proper memory. The bell ringing, swinging

from its tall, square frame, protected from the daily rain by a tiny pitched roof. Watching one of the older boys ringing the bell, pulling down so hard on the thick rope that his feet were almost lifted off the ground with each up-swing.

The bell was a constant through his early life, as constant as his parents, or his home, or his town, Agabande, with the great strangler fig tree at its centre. The boy who rang the bell would get older, and take on some new job at the seminary. An altar boy, perhaps, or later a trainee priest.

Feeling envious, and hoping that boy would one day get bored with ringing the bell every Sunday. Hoping that he might move away to the city, or even get so sick that he couldn't move. Pascal didn't want that other boy to die — not really — but he did long to be given that boy's terribly important job of ringing the bell for Jesus.

Pascal loved Jesus. Jesus loved him in return. Cared for him. Had died to save him, which is the most loving thing anyone can do for another person. That's what Jesus had done. This is what his parents said, this is what Father Michel and Father Oscar said. It was what Pascal believed. It was what he knew. He knew it better than almost anything.

His eldest brother Taribe, who had gone to study in Brussels, was the only person in Pascal's family who didn't believe in Jesus. Mama didn't like to talk about this unthinkable fact. It made her sad to talk about it, and Pascal knew this to be true, judging by the way Mama would get that certain look whenever anyone asked about Taribe.

"He's liking Brussels very much," Mama would say. "He's studying hard, and he works in a bar." But then she would clear her throat and look down at the ground, scratch her right eyebrow with her thumb. And it was time to change the subject. That's what smart people did.

Sunday. The best day of all, because of breakfast, and Sunday School. Songs and stories and smiling faces. Wide, bright smiles on shining black faces. Maybe it was because of the white cloth against black skin that everything seemed more *sensible* on Sunday. Crisp and sharp, like a clap of the hands. But Pascal also loved Sunday because the routine was different from the other six days of the week. On Sunday it *wasn't* his brother's job to wake him up.

The enjoyment Jean-Baptiste seemed to take each morning from pulling Pascal's blanket off and watching him curl up into a little, complaining ball — it just wasn't right.

He'd cackle like a crazy person, and Pascal would groan, pulling his blanket back over himself. "Get lost, or I'll tell Mama."

"Go on — I dare you. She's the one who told me to wake you up in the first place."

Six mornings a week it was this way. Pascal, waking up to something unpleasant. Sometimes cold water dripped on his face, or being dragged out of bed by his big toes until his toe-knuckles cracked. Once Jean-Baptiste put a broody hen in Pascal's bed. Another time it was a dead rat that the dog had brought inside. More than once he'd put his butt right over Pascal's face and let rip, and Pascal had woken with a terrible stench burning the inside of his nostrils.

To wake up before Jean-Baptiste, so he could do something just as bad — that would be something. But Pascal always slept too well. This was why he always woke to something awful.

But not on Sundays. Jean-Baptiste had to be up extra early on Sundays. He had a job to do, over on the other side of the valley.

Jean-Baptiste had to go and ring the church bell.

As soon as Pascal was properly awake, and while his little sister Nadine kept on snoring softly, he'd pull on his shorts and go out to the water tank to wash. Every morning was like this, even Sundays. The sun slanting golden through the banana trees behind the house and glistening off the dew on the grass. All the colours seemed so much brighter at that time of morning. The grass greener, the soil more red, the sky more blue.

And the sounds. Those early sounds. Mostly it was the rooster, Hugo. A noisy brute, standing up there on the henhouse crowing, with his head tipped way back. The red feathers around his neck puffed up, making him look twice as big. And loud! So loud! He'd just stand there and crow until all his hens were awake and gathering at the main gate. Then Pascal would set them free. They were all so serious as they charged into the yard to start their day of scratching and pecking, and it always made him smile.

Always.

Other birds, too. Tiny finches darting around in the bushes, making their little whistles and chirrups. Quail and guinea fowl and mousebirds scratching and fussing in the undergrowth while overhead a hawk or two would criss-cross the sky. Looking down, seeing everything. Watching for an opportunity.

For Pascal, that part of every morning was the same as any other. Out of bed, let out the chickens, take the goat to a new part of the garden and tie her up, just out of reach of the beans or bananas or cassava or corn. Make sure that she and the cow had clean water. Milking the cow wasn't his job — that was one of Jean-Baptiste's chores, six days a week.

When all that was done, it was time to wash his face and hands, because breakfast would soon be ready.

Breakfast. Sorghum porridge, watered-down milk. Some-times bread. Never meat. Usually sorghum.

But on Sundays, breakfast was different. They drank proper milk for Sunday breakfast. No sorghum, no watered-down milk, but the real thing. Full strength, creamy milk. They drank it from bowls, not cups. Mama always put some aside for Jean-Baptiste. After all, he was over the other side of the valley ringing the church bell.

Then, instead of getting ready for school, Pascal would pull on his white shirt and navy blue shorts and get ready to walk to church, with the sound of Jean-Baptiste's bell calling him and his family down into the valley and up the other side to the seminary church, which perched like heaven itself on top of the mist that lay heavy over the town.

This town.

Small, clinging to the bottom of the crooked valley like grime in a fingerprint. The slopes in this part of the country were steep, and the mountains were always in the edge of your view. The gorillas lived in those mountains, and the tourists came to see the gorillas. They stayed in the lodge with the tall white fence and the metal gates, and took photos of the town as they were driven through in their minibus. But they never stopped in town. They just took photos through the dusty windows of their minivans and safari trucks.

Pascal had never been to see the gorillas. He didn't know anyone who had. One of his brother's friends, Kami, said that his father was a guide, and that may or may not have been true. Pascal didn't trust anything Kami said anyway. He'd been known to lie in the past. He was a snake. Unable to be trusted. Just like his younger brother, Paul.

This town, with its handful of shops. The main street, its short section of tar the only sealed road for kilometres in any direction, the only relief from the bone-jarring ruts and potholes, a thin, ragged strip of asphalt along the middle of a much wider strip of dirt, dusty in the dry and muddy in the wet, padded free of grass and weeds by thousands of feet.

What else in the town? A bar for the grown-ups. A small grocery store opposite the school and the giant strangler fig tree on the corner of the road that led up to the seminary and its church. The medical clinic beside Mr. Ingabire's store, run by Dr. Singh and his wife, who worked as the clinic nurse. The mechanic's garage with the stacks of broken motorcycles and worn tires at the side. And behind the main row of shops was the market, a narrow, sloping lane lined with stalls and faded umbrellas, all faintly tinted with red dust and peppered with stray dogs.

Pascal's family lived high on the eastern side of the valley. From the front of their house they looked down on the roofs of the town and over the stripes of green terraces. Directly across the valley was the seminary. The church had once been white. Now, when viewed from up close, it was streaked by years of rain and red dust. But from Pascal's house it still appeared white, especially in the early morning. It stood out starkly against the bright green of the grass and trees and bushes, and when the morning mist came through the valley and settled over the town like a steaming lake, the church floated above it like a ship.

Tucked in behind the church was the seminary itself. Two classrooms, a kitchen and small dining room, the dormitory where the young trainee priests lived, Father Michel's house with his office next door. And through a steel gate in a tall red brick fence was the compound where the nuns lived and worked.

The nuns kept vegetable gardens and chickens.

The priests kept goats and some cows.

Everything was shared. But they never drank the milk they collected.

They gave it all away to the poor.

All of it.

They were servants of God, walking in Jesus' footsteps. Following his example.

Caring for the people.

All of the people.

All of the people. Men, women, children, Hutu, Tutsi, Twa.

All of them.

Agabande, Musanze District, Northern Rwanda

This morning Pascal awoke without any help from Jean-Baptiste. His brother's bed was empty. So was Nadine's. The sun was higher, the day brighter than seemed right, especially for the wet season.

The day was too bright because it was late in the morning. Too late. He'd overslept.

Pulling on his shorts and a T-shirt, he went into the kitchen.

Mama didn't look around as he came in. She just *knew*, somehow. Just knew that he was there.

"It's late," she said. "Hear that, boy? That's the rooster. He's going crazy. Him and the hens. All of them."

"Sorry, Mama."

"And the goat too, no doubt."

"Sorry, Mama."

"Why are you up so late, anyway?"

"I just slept too long."

"It's halfway to lunch."

"I know. I slept too long, that's all."

Mama turned, glared, took his chin in her hand and tilted his head back. "Are you sick?"

Pulling away. "No, I'm fine."

14

"That's good." Then she smiled. "Since you're not sick, you can go and do your chores."

"Yeah, Scally, go and do your chores!" echoed Nadine, who was sitting at the end of the table playing with some blocks of wood.

"What if I'd said I was sick?" Pascal asked Mama.

"Then I'd have got your brother to do your chores. But since you're not . . . "

Pascal coughed. "You know, maybe I do feel a bit —"

Mama cuffed him gently across the back of the head. "Too late. You told me you were fine. Go on, get on with it."

"Make sure you give Iggy a kiss, Scally!" Nadine ordered.

Pascal emerged from the house to see Papa standing in the backyard, right in the middle. He was stroking his little collection of chin-whiskers, his head tipped to one side as he stared at the old rusty water tank lying on its side on the ground next to the new one, right by the chicken run. They'd put the new tank in almost a year ago. To own a water tank was a rare thing. Most families needed to collect water from a communal pump or a standpipe. Most of Pascal's school friends had to collect water as one of their morning chores, and sometimes in the evening as well.

But when Taribe had been in Belgium for a year or so, studying at university and working at a bar, he sent some money back to Mama and Papa. It was for a water tank, he said. A water tank and nothing else. He didn't want to imagine his brothers and sister walking all the way down to the main pump in town just to get water to wash their faces in. Water to drink.

Papa tried to save some money by buying a tank that someone else didn't want any more. He and his friends rolled it up the hill, stopping when they got tired, keeping the tank in place with sandbags. It took them most of the day. By the time they got it into the yard and ready to lift onto the stand that Papa had built from mud bricks, the tank was dented and bent, and some of the rusty spots that had been painted over were beginning to split.

So he'd bought a new one. They had to wait for it to be delivered from Ruhengeri. It was a big deal, someone having a tank put in their backyard — it felt as if most of the town had turned out to watch. The truck growled up the rutted road to their house, stopped, and the driver and his three companions climbed out. "Mr. Turatsinze?"

"That's right," Papa said. "I'm taking delivery of a water tank." As if they had turned up for some other reason.

Pascal remembered the shame on Mama's face when one of the men from the truck asked her for a drink of water, once the tank was unloaded.

"I don't have any to give you," she'd said.

Papa had answered immediately, trying to lighten the mood. "But come back in a week and we'll pour you one straight out of the tank," he said.

And now, a year later, Papa was standing in the middle of the garden looking at the old tank. The one that made it to the top of the hill but never to the top of the stand.

"You're late, boy," Papa said without even glancing his way. Then he turned, saw Pascal stroking his chin and burst out laughing. "Are you copying me?"

Pascal grinned. "Maybe. What are you doing?"

"That," Papa said, pointing with his lips towards the old tank. "I'm thinking about getting rid of it."

"Why?"

"Because it's old and broken."

"What would you do with it?"

Papa shrugged. "I suppose I could get Mr. Bullo to come and take it away on his truck. Him and those three useless sons of his. That youngest one — his eye gives me the creeps." Then Papa snapped his fingers. An idea. "Oh, or maybe your friend Henri's dad could come and get rid of it for me. He does jobs like that, doesn't he?"

"What would Mr. Bullo do with the tank?"

"I don't know. Cut it up. Sell it off in bits. You could replace the roof of a small house with that much iron."

"Could he fix it?"

"*This* tank? Just look at all that rust. No, from now on this can be lots of things, but never a water tank." Suddenly he clapped his hands together. Snapping himself out of thinking-mode and into doing-mode. "All right, time to get on with your chores. Quick as you can — we've got Saturday jobs to do, and we're already late starting. Look at the rooster — he's going crazy in there."

One of the Saturday jobs was helping Papa in the garden. They'd work hard side by side until the middle of the day, then they'd have a couple of hours off while it was hot, before going back to do just a little more.

Halfway through the afternoon, or earlier if they'd made good progress, they'd pack up the gardening tools.

17

Gardening with Papa was good, even if it sometimes made Pascal's back ache. They hoed the rich, red soil, Papa's tight skin glistening with sweat as his muscles rippled underneath. From time to time Pascal would glance down at his own bare arms. Flex his biceps. Compare.

Making seed holes with the long, thin planting pole, which he would jab down into the fresh furrows. One end of a row to another, short steps, one hole per step. Papa a few steps behind him, a stack of cassava cuttings in his arms. Or a plastic bag of dried beans swinging from his hand, dropping one bean into each hole. Papa pressing the soil down over the bean with his foot. "Not too hard, but hard enough," he explained when Pascal finally was trusted to do the planting.

Such pride! He felt such pride the first time he went an entire row with his father walking in front of him, making the seed holes but not looking back to check that he was doing it right.

Of course, Jean-Baptiste was supposed to be helping too, but half the time he wasn't even in sight. "Missing in action," Papa would say, which was usually just another way of saying that Jean-Baptiste was playing soccer.

Pascal liked playing soccer too, but he didn't mind that his brother wasn't there. Not really. Jean-Baptiste would only have been causing trouble anyway. He'd never been very good at doing what he was told. Maybe he didn't care when Mama and Papa got angry, or maybe he was no good at understanding instructions. Pascal figured he only managed to ring the church bell properly because there's not much you can do wrong when you're yanking on a rope.

Of course, like a good daughter, Nadine was helping Mama. Not a lot, but she was still little. "Doing more playing than helping, but that's all right. Let her be a child for a bit longer," Papa would say, as if Pascal could do anything about it anyway. "You don't get to be a child for very long."

Too long, Pascal would think. He couldn't wait to be older. He was always checking his biceps, checking his chin for whiskers.

When the Saturday chores were done, Pascal would sometimes run off to find Henri, but many Saturday afternoons he stayed with his father. They'd go into the little shelter Papa had built on the side wall of the house, and they'd chat while Papa carved.

In a wooden box in that little shelter was an array of chisels and awls and other tools that Pascal wasn't allowed to touch. Papa would use these tools to turn lumps of wood into toys and figurines.

Birds were his favourite things to carve. He made gorillas and chimps too — that was what the tourists liked to buy — but it was the birds that he seemed to like making the best. Sometimes he rubbed them with steel wool until they were smooth and shiny like a river pebble. Other times he'd leave them just a little rough, with edges and grooves. "It's more like feathers when I do them that way," he said.

On the second Saturday of each month Papa would take his toys and figures across to Ruhengeri to sell them to the tourists who'd come to Rwanda to see the mountain gorillas. He'd wrap them individually in newspaper, pack them into two big bags and catch the bus to town. Then later that evening he'd return, sometimes with empty bags and lots of "Europe-money," sometimes full bags and very little money. It wasn't his actual job — for about a couple of years now he'd had a proper job looking after the trucks at the local government office in Ruhengeri — but he liked doing it. And he liked having a few more francs to spend on his family.

"Why do you only make birds and animals?" Pascal asked him one Saturday, when they'd been forced under cover early by a heavy rain shower.

"What else would I make?"

"Toy cars, maybe," Pascal replied. "Or dolls' furniture. You could make houses for dolls, and the furniture to put in them."

Papa brushed some shavings away from the head of the owl he'd been working on, then bent down to blow into the grooves around the neck feathers. "No. Those things are too square. They're not natural. Always the same. Angles and lines." Then Papa did one of his favourite things, which was to change the subject without really changing the subject. "Are you like your brothers and sister?"

"A bit, I guess."

"But you're not *exactly* the same as them, are you? Imagine if all people were the same. Wouldn't life be boring? Do you know what people at the market say when they pick up one of my carvings?"

"'How much?'"

Papa smiled, showing all his teeth, and the gap at the bottom. "Yes, they do say that. But they also say, 'I love how they're all so different.'"

Pascal said nothing. Not yet. There was more coming — he just knew it.

"Do you know what God created on the fourth day?"

Pascal thought back to Sunday School under the mango tree beside the church. Sister Lourdes had talked about Genesis only a few weeks before. "Was it birds?"

"Right. And the next day?"

"Animals?"

"Right. And the sixth day?"

"People, I think."

"People, yes. And what day did he make cars and furniture?"

Pascal had to think for a second or two. "He didn't."

"That's right, he didn't."

Pascal nodded. He was still thinking. "Papa?"

"Hmm?"

"If God made people on the sixth day, when did he make the Tutsi?"

Papa stopped carving. "What do you mean?" he asked, his eyes boring into Pascal's. "Why would you . . . I don't understand."

"The radio. I heard someone say that the Tutsi aren't really people. That we're less than people."

"Did they indeed?"

Pascal nodded.

21

"Tell me, my boy, are you a person?"

"Of course."

"Are your sister and brothers people? How about your mother? Is she a person?"

"Of course," Pascal said, surprised at Papa's sudden anger. This wasn't like him at all. "We all are."

"Don't listen to the radio," Papa said. "No more radio."

"But I like —" Pascal began, but Papa cut him off.

"No more radio. I forbid it." He picked up his sharpest chisel and went back to making grooves that looked just like the neck feathers of an owl. "Go and see if your mother needs any help."

"But the rain . . ."

"Go. Now."

The radio man's voice. Soft, smooth, like coffee. But with a faint bitterness to it. Like coffee.

"Today I want to talk about cleanliness in the home," the man said.

That's an odd topic, Pascal thought. Keeping the home clean? He looked around Henri's house. Dirty dishes, unwashed pots, stained rugs, empty bottles and containers and plastic bags stacked — or *almost* stacked — in the corners. Maybe it would be good if his father took the radio man's advice. But it had been like this ever since Henri's mother died, and that was maybe a year or more ago.

"No one wants pests around their home, do they?" the man went on. "Rats, mice, snails . . . cockroaches."

That last word, said with a snarl. "*Cockroaches . . .*"

"No one likes cockroaches, the way they skitter around, leaving their mess behind, getting their horrible, dirty feet all over the place."

"He's right," Henri said. "Cockroaches are disgusting."

"I know," Pascal agreed. They gave him the creeps, especially the big ones that hung around their pit toilet. Big and brown and shiny, sometimes using their wings to flutter crookedly out of the darkness. He shuddered to even think about them.

"When we have rats and mice in the house, what do we do?" the radio man asked. "We lay traps, or we get a cat or a dog, don't we? But let me tell you something — cockroaches are harder to get rid of than rats and mice. They're such dirty little things, hiding in the dark corners. And now, more than ever before, Rwanda is suffering from a cockroach plague. A *plague*, I tell you!"

"Is that true?" Pascal asked Henri. "Doesn't a plague mean that there's heaps and heaps?"

Henri shrugged. "I think so. I'm not sure."

A plague? Pascal had seen a few cockroaches about, but he'd probably seen just as many dogs wandering around the town, but no one was talking about a dog plague. Or a people plague, and there were a *lot* of people. More people than cockroaches? It was hard to say, because when they weren't trying to fly, cockroaches hid in the dark. Just the way the radio man said.

"Anyway, I don't want to say too much more on that topic," the man went on. "But at some point, something has to give."

Something has to give. Pascal turned the phrase over in his mind. Something has to give. Those words had a scary edge to them, said the way the man had said them.

"My brother Oliver says that we have way too many cockroaches around here," Henri said as he switched off the radio. "So does my dad."

Pascal glanced around the room again. He wasn't surprised to hear this latest piece of news. This place would be like heaven for a dirty old cockroach and its grubby little family.

"Do you want to go to my place?" he asked. "I want to show you what I've done to the hideout."

"Do you have whisky?"

"Of course!"

"Good. Then let's go. But I can't stay for long."

Pascal and his friend Henri in the old water tank. The entrance to their hideout was the hole in the top where the water had once run into the tank. Now, because the tank was lying down, the hole was on the side, and close to the ground. It was a tight squeeze for a small boy. No way a normal-sized adult could fit through there. But once that small boy was properly inside, the tank was high enough for him — and his friend — to stand up in.

Over several months they'd collected wooden beams and planks from around the place, taken them in there and made a floor and some rough "furniture."

One day soon they would pluck up the courage to ask their parents if they could sleep out there overnight. But that would mean telling their parents about the existence of their secret place. Which would mean that it wouldn't be secret any more. And therefore no longer a hideout.

"We're running low on kerosene," Henri said as he checked the little reservoir at the bottom of their lamp, which they'd found beside the road near the tourist lodge. It had just been lying in the ditch. The glass was cracked and had a hole on one side, but everything else was there. It hadn't been too difficult to shape some aluminium from a drink can to patch over the hole in the glass. Now that patch worked a little like a lens, reflecting and focusing the light into the darkness of the tank.

"I'll get some tonight," Pascal said. "Give me the jar."

Henri handed Pascal the kerosene jar, which he placed on the floor near the door-hole. He would need to be sneaky, but he'd taken kerosene often enough to know how to pick his times.

"Shh," he suddenly said as he heard the back door open. Someone was coming outside. Footsteps on the well-trodden little path to the outside pit toilet, which was barely five metres from their tank. The familiar squeak of the toilet door, the rattle of the makeshift latch — a wire loop that hooked over a nail at the top of the door.

A few minutes later, after a few echoing noises from the toilet that had the boys shaking with silent laughter, the latch rattled, the door squeaked, the footsteps returned to the house. The back door opened, but before they heard it close, Mama said, "It's time for your afternoon chores, Pascal. Henri can help you or go home."

After she'd gone inside, the boys burst out laughing.

"Did you hear that?" Henri giggled. Then he made a long, watery farting sound with his lips. "That was disgusting!"

"Hey! That's my mama you're making fun of!"

"You were laughing too."

"I know."

"Do you think she knows we're in here?" Henri asked.

"No, she's got no idea. More whisky?"

"Yes, please." Henri held out his small drinking jar, and Pascal poured some more of the sugar, honey and lemon water from the larger jar with *WHISKY* scratched in the side. It didn't taste the best, this "whisky," which meant that it made them screw up their faces when they drank it. It was the same face that the adults made when they drank real whisky at the bar, so it must have been close enough to the right stuff. Grown-ups did some weird things.

"So if your mama has no idea that we're in here, how did she know to just talk to us in a normal voice?" asked Henri.

"Oh, she knows we're out here somewhere. She doesn't know exactly where, that's all."

"Oh. Well, that's good."

"I'd better do my jobs. Do you want to help me?"

Henri looked at Pascal like he had several heads. "No," he said, turning out the lamp. "Dad will be home soon, and I've got my own chores to do."

"Catching cockroaches?" Pascal joked.

Henri laughed. "Maybe."

That evening, sitting in the front room. Mama stitching

buttons on a shirt. Papa sitting in his chair, rubbing oil into carved wooden gorillas with a cotton rag before wrapping them in old sheets of newspaper, crinkled and soft from being wrapped around dozens of other carvings in the past. Pascal was sitting on the floor in the corner drawing a picture of a soccer match. Red and white for his beloved Monaco. Red, blue and white for the hated Paris Saint-Germain. Except he had no red pencil, so he'd had to use an orange one instead. But it didn't matter. If he squinted at the page and used a bit of imagination, it was still Monaco versus PSG to him. Besides, the scoreboard he'd drawn in the top right corner told the true story — *MON 4: PSG 0.*

Yes, everything was just as it was supposed to be.

His brother lay on the floor with his legs up on a chair and his head tilted way back. He was humming a tune, over and over, just under his breath. Just loud enough to be annoying. It didn't seem to be annoying anyone except Pascal. Not even Nadine, who would usually have been the first to complain.

His sister was lying on her belly on one of the rugs Mama made — old dresses and shirts torn into long strips and knotted through a sheet of discarded mosquito netting. Once the colours of the cloth had been bright, but now they were faded. The strips of fabric created a perfect setting for Nadine's game. It involved several of the tiny wooden dolls Papa had carved just for her. Smaller than Pascal's pinky finger, but with arms and legs joined to the body with thread, and heads with faces carved right into them.

"Hey, Nadine," Pascal said.

She didn't hear him. She just went on doing all the voices in her game. "Stop, stop! I see you there! You can't get away! Yes I can! You're not the boss of me! I am so! You have to do what I say!"

Pascal tried again. "Nadine."

She looked up at him. *Now* she seemed annoyed. "What?"

"Your game — what's it called?"

"The People Game," she replied, as if that were the most obvious thing ever.

"And what do the people do in the People Game?"

"They live in the jungle," she answered. Then she tugged at a couple of the cloth strips. "These are big leaves. And that's where they live. They live under the big leaves."

"You know what else you could play?" said Jean-Baptiste, flipping himself around and joining Nadine on the mat. "You could play my game. It's called the Chasing Game."

"I don't want to play that," Nadine complained. "I'm playing *my* game!"

"Yes, but look," Jean-Baptiste said, grabbing a couple of Nadine's figurines. "This one is running away through the jungle, and this one is chasing him . . ."

"Stop!" Nadine squealed. "I'm playing with them!"

"I know, but your game is stupid," Jean-Baptiste said. "Check out mine! This guy is all, 'Aaargh!' and this other one is going, 'I'm gonna get you! I'm gonna get you! I'm gonna kill you!' And this one is saying, 'Please don't kill me! I'll do anything you want, as long as you don't —'"

"Jean-Baptiste!" Mama snapped. "Enough."

"But it's much more exciting than what she's playing."

"Maybe for you. But Nadine's got her own game going on. So please give her toys back to her. *Now*, thank you."

"And no talk of killing," Papa added. "Killing isn't fun."

"It's just a game," Jean-Baptiste protested.

"Killing isn't a game," Papa repeated. "Neither is running for your life."

Jean-Baptiste stood up. "I was bored anyway," he said. "I'm going to my room."

Nadine made a little grumble beneath her breath before returning all her figurines to their original positions.

"You need to talk to him," Mama said to Papa.

"I know. I will."

"Soon," she went on. "Father to son."

"About what?" Pascal asked.

"It doesn't concern you," Papa replied.

"I'm your son too."

"All right," Papa said. "All right. I'll do it. For both of you. I'll find the right time. Now, I think it's bedtime for you. Go on, go and get ready for bed."

Dropping his pencils into the cut-off plastic soft drink bottle, taking it into the bedroom he shared with his siblings.

Jean-Baptiste was lying across his bed, with his feet up on the wall. The paint was stained in that spot from years of having bare, dusty feet against it.

"You're weird," Pascal said, putting the pencils away in the little wooden box beside his bed.

Jean-Baptiste didn't even look at him. "What's weird about me?"

"It's as if you'd rather be upside down than the right way up."

"What are you talking about?"

"This — the way you're lying now. And out in the front room, lying on the floor with your feet on the chair, or swinging from the fig tree with Kami."

Jean-Baptiste folded his legs down and turned over. "You stay out of our fig tree," he said. "I'm serious."

"Which one? The big one on the corner?"

"You know which one. You and Henri stay out of it."

"Why should we? It's not your tree."

"No? Then whose tree is it?"

"It's . . . the town's tree. It's everyone's tree."

Jean-Baptiste shook his head. "It's not everyone's tree. We claimed it. Me and Kami. And some of the others."

"Kami? He's a lying snake. As if his father works at the tourist lodge!"

"He does," Jean-Baptiste said. "And his mother, too."

Pascal laughed. "As if!"

"It's true. She cleans the rooms after the Europeans and Americans have left. Kami said that she met Lothar Matthäus. And Jürgen Klinsmann."

Pascal's eyes narrowed. "Did she really?"

"That's what he said. Anyway, stay out of our tree. That's an order."

"Or what?"

"Or you'll have to live with the . . . with the stuff that happens next."

"You can't stop us climbing it," Pascal replied.

"Just don't," Jean-Baptiste warned. "Don't you dare."

"Fine, keep your stupid tree. There's lots of other trees anyway."

"Good."

"Besides, we've got our own secret hideout."

Jean-Baptiste snorted. "Sure you do."

"We do."

"Yeah? Where is it, then?"

"If I tell you —"

"Yeah, yeah, I know, it won't be a secret any more. I don't even care. Just stay out of our tree."

"Boys," said Papa from the doorway. "I need to speak with you." He came in and sat down beside Jean-Baptiste. "It's important."

Pascal searched his father's face. He looked more serious than he'd ever seen him. Not angry like he'd been when Pascal had asked what day God created Tutsis. Just serious. Very, very serious.

"Boys. Listen to me."

Even Jean-Baptiste had noticed Papa's expression.

"We're listening, Papa."

"It's about your friends. Your best friends. Kami and Henri."

In that instant, Pascal flipped through everything he and Henri had done in the last week or so. Anything bad they might have done, any rules they might have broken, and promises they might have made. He couldn't think of anything.

"Do your friends ever . . . Do they ever call you names?"

31

"Like what?" Jean-Baptiste asked. "Sometimes Kami calls me a mountain goat. He says that when I laugh I sound just like a —"

"No," Papa interrupted. "I mean, names about . . ." He stopped and burrowed around in his ear with his little finger. "Have they ever called you a cockroach or anything like that?"

"A cockroach?" Jean-Baptiste asked, frowning. "No. And even if he did, I'd just say, '*You're* the cockroach, you cockroach!'"

"Hmm," Papa replied. "And you, Pascal?"

Pascal shook his head. Like his brother's friend Kami, Henri had only ever called him playful names. Never anything hurtful. And definitely never "cockroach." That just seemed like a strange thing to call someone.

"Why, Papa?" Jean-Baptiste asked.

"It's nothing," Papa said. "Get ready for bed — it's late. And you have school tomorrow."

"No, we don't," Jean-Baptiste said. "Tomorrow's Sunday."

"Of course it is," Papa replied. "Well, it's bedtime anyway. Jean-Baptiste, you've got to ring the bell in the morning, remember? You need your rest."

Pascal smiled to himself when he heard this. His brother needed his rest? How hard could it be to ring a bell? Maybe it was harder for Jean-Baptiste than it was for normal people.

One day I'll get my turn, Pascal thought. And when I do, I'm going to ring that bell better and louder than anyone has ever rung it. That's the truth.

Agabande, Rwanda

That bell woke him the next morning. It wasn't really all that loud, from way over there on the other side of the valley, yet somehow it always broke into his dreams. Lifted him out. Picked him up by the edges.

He sat up. Jean-Baptiste's bed was empty, of course. So was Nadine's; she'd be in bed with Mama and Papa, flopping about and making Papa irritable. That was the way most nights ended, even though she'd be five in two days.

Chores first. Then breakfast. No sorghum today. Today was the day for milk, drunk from bowls. Warm cow's milk, poured from the bucket straight into the jug. And from there into the bowls. But only after Pascal had done his chores, which included trying to avoid being stepped on by Lucé the cow while he coaxed the long streams of milk from her udder into the green plastic milk bucket.

Today, Iggy wasn't where she was supposed to be. Her pen, which was made of thick sticks bound together with wire, was empty, and it took Pascal less than a minute to find the spot she'd escaped from. Several of the sticks had been broken, all around the same spot. Iggy had used her stubby little horns to break out of places before, but Papa had used much thicker sticks this time. Still not thick enough, as it turned out. So, it was time to find Iggy. From its hook beside the pen's gate, Pascal grabbed the length of rope that he used as a halter and went in search of the goat.

It didn't take long to find her. Pascal knew she'd either be in the corn patch, or eating the passion fruit flowers by the fence that they shared with the Malolos next door.

Eating flowers was where he found her. She heard him coming across the yard and raised her head to watch him approach, a half-chewed flower hanging from one side of her mouth.

"You," he said. "I'm going to have to start putting this halter on you at night as well. You won't like that, but I'll do it if you don't stop breaking out of your pen."

As he was putting the halter around Iggy's neck, Pascal heard someone on the other side of the tall, sagging fence. It was Mrs. Malolo, with her funny, squeaky little voice. "Don't look at me like that," she was saying. "You'll make me sad."

Pascal moved closer, towards a hole near the top of the fence. A hole at face height. Looking through the hole. Mrs. Malolo crouched down beside the entrance to her chicken pen. She may have even been stroking a chicken — from that angle, it was hard for Pascal to be sure.

"We can't take you with us," she was saying. "That's why we're going to let you go. I hope you lay your eggs some-where peaceful and safe." Then, as if it were answering her, a chicken made a squawk.

What a strange thing that is, Pascal thought, talking to your chickens. Then he remembered that he'd been talking to his goat a few seconds before, and felt slightly silly.

"Come on, Iggy," he said quietly, taking the halter. "Let's get you sorted out."

Iggy took one last lunge at the passion fruit vine, trying to grab one more mouthful of flowers, but Pascal gave the halter a sharp yank and, with a grunt, she followed him.

"How is my family this morning?" Papa asked, smiling around the table.

"It's Sunday," Mama said. "So it's a good day." She glanced at the two empty chairs — one for Jean-Baptiste, one for Taribe. "I wish everyone was here, but at least we're all alive and well. God is good."

"God *is* good," Papa agreed. "He's blessed us. We should pray. To give thanks."

They held hands around the table.

"Father, we thank you for your mercy and your generosity. We thank you for all that we have, and we pray for those without family, food or shelter. May you bless them as you've blessed us. In the name of the Father, Son and Holy Spirit. Amen."

They made the sign of the cross. Nadine got it horribly wrong, just as she usually did. Instead of up, down, left, right, she went left, down, left, right, down, up. Then once more on the left, just to make sure.

"No, let me show you — it's like this," Mama said, taking Nadine's hand and doing it properly. "Up, down, this side, then this side."

"Sorry, Mama," Nadine said.

"You're little," Papa said. "It's not your fault."

"I'm not that little," Nadine said. "I'll be five soon."

"Yes, you'll be five very soon," Mama said, gently cupping Nadine's cheek with her hand.

"You'll still be little," Pascal murmured.

"Will not!"

"Yes, you will be."

Papa cleared his throat. "Drink your milk. Both of you. And make sure you leave some for your brother."

"Pascal," Mama said, "thank you for milking Lucé. Did you let Hugo and the chickens out?"

"Yes."

"And Iggy?"

Pascal nodded.

"Did you give Iggy a kiss?" Nadine asked.

"Oh, but you know what?" he said, suddenly remembering. "Mrs. Malolo is letting her chickens out too."

Mama looked at him blankly. "I'm sorry, I don't . . . Why are you telling me that? I don't need to know that . . . do I?"

"I don't mean letting them out to scratch around in the garden. I mean she let them out *for good*."

Still Mama wasn't getting it. "*What* are you talking about?"

Pascal sighed. Sometimes parents found it really hard to concentrate. "She said that they're going away, and that they can't take the chickens with them. She told them to lay their eggs somewhere safe."

"That's strange . . . " Papa muttered. "Son, when did she tell you this?"

"She didn't. But I heard her say it."

"What did she say? I mean, what did she say *exactly*?"

Pascal tried to think. "She said that she was sorry they had to leave, and that they hoped they'd lay their eggs somewhere nice."

"Are you sure she was talking to the chickens?" Mama asked.

"What else has eggs?" Papa interrupted.

"Ducks have eggs," Nadine said. "So do turtles."

"I don't think the Malolos have turtles or ducks," Pascal said with a chuckle. His little sister didn't even realize how stupid she could be sometimes.

But Mama and Papa weren't even paying attention to how stupid his sister was being. They were just having one of their silent conversations. The ones where they didn't say a word, but still managed to talk about all kinds of things, with just the use of their eyebrows.

Suddenly Papa pushed his chair back and stood. "Pascal, Nadine, drink your milk and get dressed for Mass. Do whatever your mother tells you to do."

And then he was gone out the front door.

After breakfast, Pascal returned to his room. Mama had folded back his mosquito net and laid out his special Sunday clothes on his bed. Just as she did every Sunday.

White shirt, with a collar. Navy blue shorts. No shoes. No need for shoes.

Nadine, all in white. A special dress, just for church. No shoes.

Mama. A white dress, and an *icyanganga* for her head. No shoes.

Papa, white shirt, black tie, black trousers. And shoes. White ones, Adidas. White, with three thin green Adidas stripes. Only for Sunday. They came out of the box, and after church they went straight back in the box, after being wiped clean with a damp rag.

Sunday shoes, bought with Europe-money.

Those Adidas shoes were placed side by side at the front door, waiting for Papa to return from the Malolos'.

Pascal, Nadine and Mama sat in the front room, waiting there with the white Adidas Sunday shoes.

After a while, and after Nadine had asked for the fifth or sixth time if it was time to go yet, Mama sighed. "Pascal, if you'd like to go ahead, I don't mind. At least one of us can be on time. Oh, here he is," she said as the front door opened and Papa came inside.

Papa looked straight at Mama. Their eyes met. Pascal saw him twitch his eyebrows, just the smallest bit, and Mama's mouth twisted slightly to one side. Then she scratched her forehead with her thumb.

"What's happening?" Pascal asked.

"Nothing," Papa replied. "So, are we ready?"

"Just waiting for you to put your fancy shoes on," Mama said.

So shoes on, and they were ready to go. Papa with his Bible, Mama with her purse. Something in it for the collection, but not much else.

From their front door, the church was floating like a white ship above the last of the morning mist. The bell rang like a fog warning. The young priests and nuns drifted towards the church in their lines, like gulls following a fishing boat.

Down the crooked red path from their house, greeting others on their way to church. All dressed up and looking special. All washed and smiling. White smiles in black faces. Hugs, happy greetings. Families holding hands, children running ahead, being called back. "Slow down — you'll fall over! You'll get your Sunday dress all muddy!"

To the bottom of the valley, down into the clearing mist. From the rutted red road on to the asphalt stained orange along the edges with the mud left there by tires and countless steps. More people joining the procession. More hugs, more shining faces, more kids running ahead.

"Wait for us at the top! And remember, don't fall over!"

Past Jean-Baptiste's strangler fig tree and up the long, less crooked road to the top of the hill on the church side of the valley. The bell getting louder. The road growing more crowded. Occasionally having to step down into the roadside grass to let a car or a small truck go by.

Past the turnoff to Henri's house.

Pascal looked up that road. Just as he did every Sunday, he hoped to see his friend trotting down from his house, coming to church. But he wouldn't be. Since his mother had died, Henri and his father hadn't been to church at all. Her funeral had been the last time.

That day. The wailing of the women. The chanting and singing of the men. The anguished, disbelieving face of Henri's father. The blank expression on Henri's. It was as if he hadn't been told that his mother had died.

But he had.

He had been told.

And he never wanted to come back to that place again, the place where he said goodbye to his mother for the last time.

Mass was joyful. Joyous. A celebration. Jesus had died so people didn't have to. Well, not forever, anyway. It was this that made Pascal saddest when he thought about Henri's mother — that if Henri and his father and Henri's elder brother Oliver didn't keep coming to church even after she'd died, they might not go to heaven when *they* died. And it was pretty simple — if they didn't go to heaven, they'd never see her again. At all. Ever. For eternity. Which was, as Father Michel liked to say, "the longest time you can think of, repeated for as many times as the largest number you can possibly imagine."

To Pascal, that felt like a very long time. Way too long to never see your mother again.

First came Sunday School. While the adults gathered together, one of the nuns, usually Sister Berenice or Sister Lourdes or sometimes Sister Odette, would take the children to the mango tree that stood beside the chapel. A song, perhaps two. A story from the nun, about Jesus performing a miracle, or Jonah being swallowed by an enormous fish, perhaps Saul being made blind by angels. Then came the lesson. Very short.

Today was the story of Balaam and his donkey. Balaam was riding his donkey when an angel — quite possibly the same one that made Saul go blind — stood on the path, right in the way of the donkey, and told it to stop. The donkey did stop. Balaam wasn't pleased. He told the donkey to start walking. The donkey refused. So Balaam hit the donkey with a stick. He hit it hard, again and again and again.

Finally the donkey had had enough, and it spoke. (The children gathered in the shade of the mango tree's broad leaves found this part of the story completely hilarious. A donkey, speaking? What craziness!)

When the donkey spoke, it asked Balaam a question. "Why are you hitting me? Have I ever done anything to you? Have I ever hit you with sticks or kicked you in the ribs?"

"No," Balaam replied.

"Then don't do it to me."

Pascal didn't hear the moral of the story. This was because the very last thing he heard was Sister Lourdes saying, " . . . so the moral of this story is what? Anyone?" before his mind wandered off. He was thinking about Iggy with the halter around her neck, asking him a question. "Have I ever put you in a cage for the night? Have I ever put a loop of rough rope around your neck and dragged you away from the tastiest passion fruit flowers any goat in the history of goats has ever been lucky enough to taste?"

It was a thought that made him smile, right up to the moment a small stick bounced off his cheek. Yves, a boy Pascal had never really liked very much, had thrown a twig at his face. "Hey! Wake up."

"What's that?" Pascal asked, when he saw that Sister Lourdes and all the other kids were staring at him, waiting for him to answer the question. But what question?

"Um . . ." he said.

Sister Lourdes shook her head slowly at Pascal. She seemed disappointed in him. "It doesn't matter," she said.

"He wouldn't have known the answer anyway," said Yves. Then, under his breath, he added something: "Stupid . . ." followed by another word that Pascal couldn't quite make out. But Yves' friend heard it clearly enough, because he started to laugh. And not just a little, chuckling laugh, but a proper, out-loud laugh.

Sister Lourdes didn't scold Yves or his friend. She simply clucked her tongue and gave them a fierce stare. Finally, when they'd realized that they could never win a staring contest with Sister Lourdes, they stopped laughing and stared at the ground instead.

She cleared her throat. "Now, before we go inside the church for Mass, we need to offer our own prayer. And today I'm going to pray for peace, understanding and acceptance . . ."

Then it was into the church for Mass. Finding Mama and Papa, who always sat in the same row. On the left, fourth row from the front. Papa next to the aisle, then Nadine, then Mama, then Pascal, and finally Jean-Baptiste.

Music. Singing, without any accompaniment from a piano or an organ or even a guitar. Just singing, loud and bold, filling the room, the women's voices rising to the ceiling, the men's voices low and resonant, swelling at the right time to fill the spaces the women's voices couldn't reach.

The Lord's Prayer. Forgive our sins just as we forgive

those who sin against us. Lead us safely through the darkest places and the darkest times. Father Michel leading the prayer, his head tipped back slightly and his face expressionless as he watched the congregation recite the words. His congregation. His sheep, or were they his goats?

Then came the sermon, which tended to be quite short. Pascal didn't always listen very closely to the sermon. It was usually full of boring bits and Bible verses. In fact, he spent most of his time looking around — at the pictures hanging on the walls of African Jesus and his African disciples, at the crucifix on the wall behind the altar, or the purple sash that Father Michel kissed and placed around his neck just before he offered the sacrament. The plate of wafers, which always made him think about lunch.

Later, after the sacrament, the people would turn to greet those in the other rows. Turning round, shaking hands, leaning forward, friendly hugs.

"God be with you."

"And also with you."

"Thank you, brother."

"God bless you, my sister."

And after all that, leaving the church. Small groups chatting and laughing, some on the front steps, some on the lawn or the red earth of the road that led through the white gate and down to the town. Men shaking hands but then hanging on loosely as they spoke. Women too, smiling, talking, sharing stories as children ran around, chased each other, climbed the Sunday School mango tree, ducked in and out of the long line of shrubs that hid the priests' dormitory from the eyes of the congregation.

And finally, the groups began to move back towards town, still talking, breaking up into smaller and smaller groups, families, men from several families together while the women from those same families walked a short distance behind. Calling out to the younger children to keep up, to come along now. Calling out to the older children to make sure they weren't late for lunch.

And the churchyard emptied, and went back to being seminary grounds, and the empty town went back to being the town, with a store and a market and a car repair shop and a clinic and a school and houses and people, Hutu and Tutsi.

In Agabande, life just carried on.

But in Agabande, something was changing.

Monday 15 March 1999

It sounds like your town — what was its name again ...?

Agabande. It sounds a bit like *akabande*, which means "small valley." I guess that's where the name came from.

Well, it sounds like Agabande was a lovely place to live.

It was. I liked it.

And your family. It was a happy family?

Yes, it was. Very happy.

Apart from fighting with your brother, that is. But that's how brothers are, right — always fighting?

I guess.

And also happy apart from your brother being in Belgium.

Yes, but in the end it was good he was in Belgium. It meant he was safe when all the bad things happened.

Yes, I suppose that's true. Pascal, I especially like the way you speak about church ... You enjoyed going to church?

I told you, Sunday was the best day of all.

Did you have a lot to do with the church? I mean, you talked about your brother ringing the bell, and how you wanted to ring the bell one day, but did you do anything else in the church? Were you an altar boy, for example?

No, I wasn't an altar boy. But there was one person from the seminary that I liked to hang out with.

If you like, you can tell me about him next time.

Next time?

Sure. Monsieur Baume wants me to keep seeing you — or for you to keep seeing me ... Let me start again: Monsieur Baume would like us to keep having these chats each lunchtime. You can get your lunch from your bag or from the canteen or whatever, and bring it with you. We can eat lunch together, if you like. You don't mind me eating tuna, do you? Because I have tuna almost every day.

I don't care what you eat. But how long will we be having lunch together to talk about all this ... stuff?

Until I'm happy, I suppose.

Until *you're* happy? I thought *I* was meant to be the one getting happier.

No, what I mean is ... You're right. Monsieur Baume wants us to keep chatting until I'm *satisfied* that you're okay. But at least until the end of the —

I told you, I'm okay.

When *I'm* satisfied about that, then you'll be okay. And then we can stop. Is that all right?

I guess. What are you writing down there?

I'm just making a note to ask you about the person from the seminary that you liked to spend time with. So, tomorrow, at a quarter to one?

Do I get a choice?

Honestly? No.

Then I guess I'll see you at a quarter to one.

How are you today, Pascal?

Good, I guess. I don't feel like being here, though. Sorry, but that's how I feel.

I understand. Did you bring your lunch?

I ate already.

What did you have?

Um . . . a bread roll and some cheese. And a bottle of juice. Why?

No reason.

No reason? You must have had a reason.

I just think it's important to have a good lunch. It makes it a lot harder to learn if you're hungry. Breakfast, too. You've got to have a good breakfast.

Did *you* have a good breakfast this morning?

Me? Well . . . probably not a good breakfast, no. I had a coffee on the way to work, and when I got to school I had another.

So why are you telling me about eating properly if —

You make a good point, Pascal. You're right. So anyway, let's get back to what we were talking about yesterday.

What were we talking about? I've forgotten.

It was Sunday. You'd just finished telling me about church and Mass. Sunday, and what it was like.

Oh, yes. Except what I was telling you was how Sunday *usually* went. But this Sunday was a bit different.

Agabande, Rwanda

This Sunday was different, but it wasn't one thing that made it so. It was a whole lot of things, and nothing. A mood. A feeling. A change that was subtle and menacing, like a mosquito in the dark.

Partly it was the stern look Father Michel gave the congregation, and the way he paused before he began his sermon. He paused so long that Pascal felt sure that he was peering into every black face in that church. He *definitely* peered into Pascal's. A child who was complaining on the other side of the church made a bit of a noise, then stopped, suddenly, as if a tap had been turned off.

Father Michel's voice was stony still and quiet as he began to speak. But every word could be heard clearly.

"In the Lord's Prayer as we just recited it, we ask God to protect us through our dark and difficult times. He promises to do that, no matter how hopeless any situation might be. We should never forget that."

Pascal glanced at Papa. He was sitting bolt upright, his hands folded in his lap, his eyes straight ahead. Stern. Listening closely.

Father Michel went on. "Our country is in turmoil, and as you know, I don't like to bring politics into the pulpit.

50

But I feel that I need to say this: it feels as though dark times are just around the corner. Hatred is growing. Brother against brother. Neighbour against neighbour. People casting angry glances, others casting suspicious ones in return. We need to remember what Jesus said — that we must love our neighbours. He didn't say which neighbours we must love. He simply said, 'Love your neighbour as yourself.' It's very clear."

He paused, looked around again. Taking everyone in. Letting his words hang until they drifted away. But then, when they had finally gone, he went on, his next words stark against the fresh silence.

"As Christians, we have that promise from God himself. From Jesus himself. And for us, as Christians, we have the knowledge that our God, our community, this very church itself, is a refuge in times of trouble. Of course we hope it never comes to that, but who knows the future, apart from Almighty God?"

Pascal looked at Nadine. She wasn't listening. Even if she had been, she probably wouldn't have understood. But Mama — she understood. She was biting the nail on the finger of one hand, scratching her eyebrow with the thumbnail of the other. Taking a deep breath. Then Pascal saw her reach across in front of Nadine and grip Papa's hand. Their eyes met. They held the look for a long moment.

It said so much. But at the same time, it didn't actually explain anything much at all.

This Sunday, something felt different out in the churchyard after Mass. Pascal couldn't quite say what it was. It felt a little like the moment right after someone blurts out some embarrassing thing at dinner, and no one quite knows what to say. The sermon seemed to have taken a lot of the joy out of the day, and even when people had turned to one another to offer God's blessings for the week ahead, there'd been something missing. Maybe their eyes hadn't met for as long as they usually did. Or the smiles were less broad. Or the eyes didn't smile with the lips. An uncomfortable heaviness hung in the air.

Outside, Pascal was on his way to climb the mango tree with some of the other kids when he felt a hand on his shoulder.

"Pascal, I haven't seen you at all this week," said Father Oscar, the junior priest who Pascal liked best. "Aren't you my friend any more?"

"I'm sorry," Pascal replied, because he was. "I've been busy."

"Of course. We're all busy. But I've missed talking to you. I always enjoy our chats."

"Me too," Pascal replied. Father Oscar was kind, like most of the priests, but he listened more than he spoke, which was very different from many of the others. He also had one hand that was slightly smaller than the other, all wizened up like the claw of a dead bird. Whenever Pascal looked at that hand for too long or thought too hard about it, he got the creeps.

But then he'd look at Father Oscar's face, and the creeps would go away.

"Pascal, we're going home," Mama called. She and Papa had Nadine by one hand each, and Nadine was lifting her feet and swinging between them. She was getting too old, too heavy, and Pascal could see that Papa wasn't enjoying the game. But he wasn't going to snap at her or grumble — that wasn't his way. Not with Nadine, at least. His princess.

"Mama, can I come later?" Pascal called back.

"No, come now. We'll be eating soon. We always eat together as a family on Sunday, remember?"

Of course he remembered. Every Sunday of his life had been the same.

"Can I bring Henri along for lunch?"

Mama didn't answer straight away. Instead, she glanced across at Papa, who nodded. A tiny nod, almost too small to be seen. But it was there, and Pascal spotted it.

"All right," Mama replied. "He's not here, is he? Go to his house and ask him if he wants to eat with us, but then come straight home, all right? Even if he says no."

"Yes, Mama."

"We'll see you at home."

"So, Pascal," Father Oscar went on. "Will you promise to visit me this week?"

"Yes," Pascal promised. "I definitely will. Tomorrow after school?"

"Very good. I'll look forward to it."

Henri's house was a small two-roomed cottage made of red mud brick, with two windows in the front and a view across the mottled green terraces of the hills surrounding Agabande. As Pascal arrived, Henri was sitting on the concrete block that served as the front doorstep. He was bending wire using a long piece of wood with a hole drilled in one end of it. Twisting, bending, folding the wire.

"Working on your tractor?" Pascal said.

Henri glanced up. "Nearly done, I think."

He'd been working on his tractor for weeks now. It didn't look much like a real tractor — it was actually a long pole with a crosspiece at the end that acted like an axle, and two carved wooden wheels. The long part of the pole would rest on the "driver's" shoulder, and another crosspiece halfway along was held like a set of handlebars. Turning the handlebars caused the axle to twist, which provided steering. Henri was going farther. He was using his wire to create a steering wheel. He'd twisted it around and around itself until it was like a thick rope, and now he was working on a way to attach it to the pole.

"Can I have a go when you're done?" Pascal asked. "All I've got on mine are motorbike grips."

"I like your motorbike grips," Henri said. "But I think my steering wheel is going to be amazing."

"I know. That's why I want a go."

"When I've had plenty of turns myself," Henri said. "Just so you know."

"Do you want to come to my house for lunch?" Pascal asked. "I already checked with Mama."

He was surprised at how quickly Henri reacted. He stood straight up and shoved his tractor and its half-constructed steering wheel through the open front window of the house. "Let's go," he said. "I'm ready."

"Shouldn't you ask your dad?"

"Nope." Henri was already walking towards the crooked little path that led down to the road itself. "If I ask him whether I can come to your house, he'll say I can't go. So if I don't ask him, he can't say no."

Pascal was trotting after him. "Won't he be mad when you get home?"

"I'll just tell him that I was down at the creek, or hanging out with Paul."

"Paul? Why would you tell him that? You hate that guy!"

"He's not too bad," Henri said.

"Why not just tell him that you were at my house?"

"Oh, yeah!" Henri said, laughing. "Of course, I'll just tell him that. He'll be fine. It'll be fine."

A lie. A lie that Henri had been *planning* to tell. The worst kind of lie — not the kind where you're put in a spot and you have to come up with something in a hurry. When people told lies like that they could go to church and confess. Confess the lie they'd told, ask for forgiveness, do their penance, promise to try harder next time. It worked the same way with any sin — confess, ask to be forgiven, do penance, promise to try to be better.

But this lie — Pascal knew Henri had no intention of telling his father he'd been at Pascal's house. It was hurtful, and it was confusing.

The boys reached the wide, busy main road in town, by the school. Across the intersection was the medical clinic, and beside it Mr. Ingabire's shop. Flat-roofed, its outside walls painted a bright blue-green that almost hurt your eyes, with tin signs nailed up where the windows had once been.

The signs were like a crazy, random patchwork, giving the impression that Mr. Ingabire's store mostly sold bits of Eveready batteries, slices of Goodyear tires, half-cans of Mobil engine oil, and very small portions of Pepsi.

Here were three of the other people in town who didn't go to church — Dr. and Mrs. Singh, and Mr. Ingabire. The Singhs didn't go to church because they weren't Christians. There was talk that Mr. Ingabire didn't go because he was an atheist, although Pascal could never work out if he opened his shop on Sunday because he didn't believe in God, or if he didn't believe in God so he could open his shop on Sunday.

Dr. Singh had a more impressive beard than any of the African men. African men tended to have smaller, patchier hair on their faces, while Dr. Singh had his beard pulled up on either side of his face and tucked into his turban. Mama said that even though the Singhs weren't Christian, they were good people who probably had their own way of asking for forgiveness, so they'd most likely be in heaven too. Maybe not the same heaven as the Catholics, but definitely *some* kind of heaven. Unlike Mr. Ingabire, who would be in hell with all the dirty money he'd made on Sundays.

Dr. Singh was painting the window frames on the clinic as Pascal and Henri crossed the road, dodging the cars, flat-top trucks and motorbikes that groaned and sputtered through the town.

"Good morning, Dr. Singh," Pascal called as they reached the far edge of the orange-tinged asphalt.

Dr. Singh looked around and up and around some more,

as if the voice had come out of the air immediately surrounding his head. For a moment, Pascal wondered if his
turban muffled or confused the sound in some way.

"Ah!" said Dr. Singh, seeing the boys at last. "Good
morning! Pascal, is it Nadine's birthday today?"

"Not tomorrow but the next day," Pascal replied.

"Well, make sure you offer her our congratulations,"
Dr. Singh said.

"I will," Pascal replied, even though he wasn't quite sure
what congratulations were.

"And tell your father I still owe him for fixing my van.
Maybe you can all come here for dinner one night. Last
time was fun, so we should do it again anyway. Make sure
you tell him, won't you?"

"I will. See you later, Dr. Singh."

"Bye, boys."

But Henri said nothing — not until they were well out
of earshot.

"*That's* the guy I *really* hate," Henri muttered.

"Dr. Singh? Why?"

"Because he killed my mother."

"Oh, I don't think that's right," Pascal said. "I thought he
tried to save her life."

"Yeah, he might have *tried* to save her life, but he didn't
actually save it, did he? So . . ."

"It wasn't his fault that she got malaria. You're talking
like he keeps mosquitoes in a jar and —"

"Hey, shut up," Henri said. "Do you want me to come to
your house or not?"

"I do. But you don't have to be mean about Dr. Singh. Ow!" he said as something hard bounced off his forehead. He'd barely had time to see the small yellow guava rolling up the road when another one hit him, this time on the fleshy part of the shoulder. "Ow! What's going on?"

"It's an ambush!" Henri shouted, ducking out of the way as another guava flew harmlessly past the side of his head and split into several pink and yellow fragments across the asphalt. "It's coming from the fig tree!"

"I bet it's Jean-Baptiste and Kami! Take cover!" Dodging a passing motorbike, Pascal made a dash for the other side of the street, Henri close behind, heading for the refuge of the narrow lane beside Mr. Ingabire's store.

"You and you. Stop." Mr. Ingabire was standing in their way, broom in hand.

Pascal stopped, while Henri only managed to slip on the dusty surface of the road and fall on to his knees. He winced and grabbed at his right knee, which had lost the top layer of skin and was already specking with blood.

"You too," Mr. Ingabire called across the road. "You, up in the tree. Yes, I can see you. Look at this mess. I've just finished sweeping this step, and making the front of my place tidy, and here you are throwing fruit all over the place. Come on, down you come. Clean up this mess."

"Sorry, Mr. Ingabire," Jean-Baptiste called.

A moment or two later he emerged from behind the vine-tangled trunk of the fig tree and crossed the street, followed by Kami. They didn't even meet Mr. Ingabire's eyes as they went around and picked up all the pieces of guava, darting between the people and the traffic.

"You missed some," Mr. Ingabire said, pointing with his broom. "And over there."

"You could help, you know," Jean-Baptiste muttered to Pascal as he came close by, picking up pieces of guava and collecting them in the front of his T-shirt.

"Why should I help? You and Kami threw them, so why should we . . ." Pascal's voice trailed off as he was distracted by the three men who'd walked up to the door of the shop. Two of them were carrying long knives. Machetes, like the one Papa used to cut the grass and small trees around their house.

The third man didn't have a machete. All he had was a long stick, like a slightly crooked walking stick, knotty at the top end.

"Ingabire, what's going on here?" asked the man with the stick. "Got the insects cleaning up?"

"Not now, Clement," Mr. Ingabire replied. "All right, that's enough," he said to the boys. "Get out of here before I tell your parents what you've been up to."

"But all we were doing —" Pascal began, but Mr. Ingabire waved him away.

"Go. And don't come back for a week."

"He always says that," Henri muttered as they walked away. "My dad says he'll take anyone's money at any time, no matter how dirty it is. I'll bet he's a cockroach."

Sunday lunch. Chicken stew and rice. Pascal watched Henri's face as Mama uncovered the serving dishes on the table. He was practically drooling. That makes sense, Pascal thought — if my mother died, I think her cooking would be what I missed most.

"Now then . . . " Papa said as he reached down by his chair and produced a long-necked bottle of Primus, which he placed on the table. He seemed triumphant as he looked around at the family. Proud. So proud it seemed as if his chest might pop.

"Beer?" said Jean-Baptiste. "What's that for? Why do you have beer, Papa?"

"To celebrate."

"Celebrate what? It's Sunday."

"Is Tee-bee coming home?" Nadine asked, which made Mama scratch her eyebrow with her thumb.

"No, your brother's not coming back from Belgium," Mama said.

"Then what?" asked Jean-Baptiste, as if Taribe coming back to visit was the only thing that could possibly be big enough news to deserve beer at lunchtime on a Sunday.

"I know," Pascal said. "The lodge."

"Then what?" asked Jean-Baptiste. "If it's not Taribe, what is it?"

"When *is* Tee-bee coming home?" asked Nadine. "I miss Tee-bee."

"We all do," said Mama.

"Then what is it?" asked Jean-Baptiste again.

"It's the lodge, isn't it?" Pascal said. "They want more carvings."

"Can I have some beer?" Jean-Baptiste picked up the

bottle of Primus, but Mama took it from his hand and deposited it firmly back on the table.

"No, absolutely not. Don't be silly."

"Is Tee-bee bigger than me or littler than me?" asked Nadine.

"Bigger, stupid. Much, much bigger," Jean-Baptiste snapped. "You're so dumb, you know that?"

"Jean-Baptiste! Don't speak that way to your sister!"

Pascal tried again. "It's the lodge, isn't it, Papa?"

"Yes, Pascal. It's the lodge," Papa replied, reaching across and squeezing his hand. "They want more of my carvings."

Meanwhile the others continued their loud and pointless argument about why Taribe was "bigger" than Nadine, and why Jean-Baptiste being "bigger" than his sister didn't mean he could talk to her however he liked. Henri sat there silently, perhaps embarrassed, but probably amused.

"How many did they say they'd take?" Pascal asked Papa.

"Lots! Four of the big gorillas, four of the silverbacks, three of the big chimps, and they said they want as many of the small gorillas as I can make."

"That's so good!"

Papa's eyes were shining with pride. "It's *so* good. And I've got so much to do."

"I'm proud of you, Papa."

"Thank you, son."

"That's good, Mr. Turatsinze," Henri said. "I hope you sell heaps."

"Thank you, Henri."

"Maybe you'll need some help," Pascal suggested.

61

"Maybe I will."

"How much do you pay?"

Papa just winked.

"So, Papa, if you're having beer to celebrate, what are us kids having?" asked Jean-Baptiste, who seemed to have lost interest in the argument about Taribe.

"Why should you have anything?" Papa asked.

But his tiny, crooked smile gave him away.

"What did you get for us kids?" Jean-Baptiste asked again. Then he bent down and checked under the table.

"Oh, all right," Papa said, and from behind his back he took a bottle of Coca-Cola. Not large. Quite small, in fact. But the real thing, with the glass all contoured and rippled around the black liquid, the white lettering on the side, the red cap. "Enough for each of you to have a decent taste," Papa said. "Pascal, get the glasses."

Five glasses from the kitchen. Mismatched glasses from the shelf beside the blue plastic washing-up tub.

"Argh!" he said as a big dark brown cockroach scuttled along the angle where the shelf met the wall. "I hate those things!"

"What is it?" Mama called.

"A cockroach. A huge one! Where's the Jolt?"

"There's a can on the windowsill. Don't waste it — just hit the cockroach with one blast if you can."

Pascal grabbed the can of Jolt. Bright yellow, with a picture of a pale blue lightning bolt turning some kind of bug into a skeleton. But by the time he got back to the shelf, the cockroach was gone.

"Did you get it?" Mama asked.

"No, it's gone. Sorry."

"It doesn't matter. Just bring the glasses."

"But now there'll be thousands of filthy cockroaches," Pascal said as he went back to the table with the glasses stacked together. "If you don't get them when you can, those disgusting creatures breed and breed and breed —"

"Pascal," Papa said, his voice suddenly cold. "Just bring the glasses and —"

"I am."

"Don't talk back, boy. Just sit down, be quiet and drink your Coca-Cola."

Pascal and Henri in their water tank hideout, drinking their whisky. It was making Pascal feel a bit ill, if he had to be honest. A cup of plain water would have been nice.

"Wait here," he said, and he slipped out of the little round door, grabbed a plastic bucket from beside the back door and took it to the new tank, the one being used properly.

He filled the bucket and carried it back to the hideout. "Here, take this," he ordered, and Henri managed to get the bucket inside without spilling too much of the water.

"What's that for?" Henri asked after Pascal had followed the bucket into the tank.

"It's water. It's for drinking."

"But we've got whisky."

"You can't drink just whisky," Pascal said. "Papa says that drinking alcohol is something you should only do to celebrate."

"What are the guys at the bar in town celebrating?" Henri asked. "Most of them look like they've never had any good luck at all. And my dad, too. He drinks when he's not celebrating. He'll have something to celebrate soon, though. Oliver's coming home."

"That's great!" Pascal said. "Is he still living in Kigali?"

"I think so."

"Are you excited?"

"I'm *so* excited." Henri's eyes glinted in the light from the lamp. "I haven't seen him for ages."

Pascal remembered when Oliver went to the capital. He remembered staying overnight at Henri's house one night shortly after his brother left, and the way Henri had tried to change the subject from Oliver to . . . well, anything else. And he remembered that later, after the lights had been turned out, Henri had kept sniffing in the darkness for a long time.

"Are you okay?" he'd asked, just trying to help, but Henri's answer had been short.

"Of course I'm okay. Shut up and go to sleep," he'd snapped in a voice that didn't sound okay at all.

And now Oliver was coming home, and Henri *would* be okay.

"I forget why he went to Kigali," Pascal said. "Was it the . . . the army, or something like that?"

"Um . . . I think so," Henri said. "Dad says it's like the army, but they get to wear different clothes."

"Like plainclothes police, except soldiers?" Pascal suggested.

"I think so. Maybe."

"That sounds pretty cool."

"I know. I'm going to do that when I'm grown up."

Just then the hinges on the back door squeaked. They continued to squeak, just the smallest bit, but there were none of the usual sounds you'd expect if it closed.

A man's voice. "Henri. It's time to go."

"It's my dad," Henri whispered. "Don't say anything."

Again. "Henri. It's time to go. Come on, boy."

Pascal's heart, thumping in his chest. "Are you in trouble?" he asked Henri, also in a whisper.

"Probably."

The hinges were still squeaking. It seemed that Henri's father was standing in the doorway, holding the door open.

"They're out there somewhere," Pascal heard Mama say. "But I'm not sure where. I hope you didn't mind Henri coming over here for lunch — I just assumed he'd asked you and you were happy for him to —"

"Henri," his father called again. "I'm going home now. Catch up to me before I get home, or there'll be big trouble. *Bigger* trouble."

Then the door squeaked once more, but this time Pascal heard it close properly.

"Oh boy," Henri sighed. "I'd better go."

"Will you be all right?"

"Yeah, I'll be fine. I'll see you later."

Later, as Pascal lay in bed waiting for sleep to come, Papa came in to say good night. First he went to Nadine, lifted her mosquito net, kissed her on the head and tucked the net back in. Just like every night.

Next was Jean-Baptiste. The same thing.

"Good night, my boy. Said your prayers?"

Jean-Baptiste murmured something.

"Make sure you do."

Then Papa was standing beside Pascal's bed. He untucked the mosquito net and bent down. His face was a dark, featureless shape. "Are you still awake?"

"Yes, Papa."

"Said your prayers?"

"I will."

"Make sure you do. Son, that thing that you said about the thousands of cockroaches breeding . . . Where did you hear that?"

"I don't know."

"I told you, no radio."

"I didn't —"

"No radio, son. Do you hear me?"

"Yes, Papa."

"No good will come of listening to the radio. Not these days. And Henri . . . I'm not sure if it's such a good idea —"

"He's my best friend, Papa."

"I know. It's just . . . It's just that our families are quite different. I don't mind that, but his father doesn't seem to think much of us."

"Maybe he's still sad because his wife died and Oliver went to Kigali," Pascal said. "But it'll be okay, because Oliver's coming home soon."

"That's good," Papa replied. Then he kissed Pascal on the forehead. Pascal smelt beer faintly on his breath. "Good night, my boy. You know I love you, don't you?"

"Of course, Papa."

"Don't forget. Ever."

"I won't."

"Mama will be in soon to say good night. Sleep well."

"Papa. I'm excited for you. About the lodge, and the carvings."

"Thank you, son." Pascal couldn't see Papa's face in the darkness, but he could hear the smile in his voice. "And you know, I might need some help, like you said."

"I'd like that," Pascal said.

"Me too."

Papa stood up and tucked the mosquito net back in. But moments after he'd left the room, Pascal heard it. The high, piercing whine of a mosquito, trapped inside the net. Trapped in there with him.

He pulled his sheet up higher, right under his chin. Then he pulled it even higher, right up over his head. No mosquito was going to get him. He was under the protection of his sheet.

And nothing protected like a sheet.

Agabande, Rwanda

What a way to wake up! Dreaming that you're standing in front of the pit toilet, trying to make yourself pee. Then starting to go, and almost immediately feeling the warmth running through your shorts and down your legs, across your belly, everywhere but into the dark hole in the ground that it's meant to be going into.

Waking up, finding that one of your hands is wet, but it's not wet with pee. It's wet with water. Warm water, in a plastic bowl lying on the bed beside you.

Pascal sat up, threw back his covers, and saw that yes, he'd wet the bed. He was lying in the middle of a dark, damp patch. He could see it very clearly, thanks to the morning light streaming through the window.

A chuckle from outside the bedroom door. A very quiet chuckle. His brother.

"I hate you!" Pascal leapt out of bed and ran at the door, heard his brother make an amused, slightly alarmed noise. "You'd better watch your back, because I'm going to get you for this!"

Out of the bedroom, around the corner, into the kitchen. Nadine was already at the table, waiting for breakfast. Mama was standing beside the cooker, mixing the sorghum porridge.

"Boys!" Mama snapped. "Boys, stop! Have you done your morning jobs?"

Jean-Baptiste turned, pointed at the dark patch that took up most of the front of Pascal's shorts. "Pascal hasn't done all his jobs, but he's made a start!" Then he laughed like mad at his own joke.

"He made me wet the bed!" Pascal complained, and Nadine giggled.

Mama seemed less amused. She raised the wooden stirring spoon from the pot. Globs of pale grey-brown porridge hung from the end. "I'll smack you with this spoon if you don't get moving," she warned.

"But then you'll get sorghum all over everything," Jean-Baptiste answered.

"Yes, but mostly you." Mama narrowed her eyes at him. "Do you really think I care about a bit of porridge if it means I get to smack you on the butt?" She was struggling to stop the smile that was already beginning to twitch at the corners of her mouth. "Go on, you cheeky things, get on with your jobs. School's in less than an hour."

First a change of pants, then outside, into the slanting golden light.

Hugo was already up, strutting about the chicken enclosure like he owned it. Iggy was in her pen, with her head stuck through the wooden poles. Busting to get out to the garden.

"Wait," Pascal said. "I have to wash myself first."

He heard Jean-Baptiste chuckle. Oh man, how he hated that sound!

"Shut up," he said. "You got me — now shut up. And don't forget, one day I'm going to —"

"Yes, you told me already — you're going to make me pay. Just go and do your jobs. The *rest* of your jobs, I mean."

Jean-Baptiste's main morning chore was milking Lucé, who was standing in her little mud brick shelter looking mournful. Pascal was glad to have other things to do instead. He'd seen far too many cow pats dropped beside the bucket. They really spattered when they hit the ground. Once he'd seen Lucé dump a stream of warm green poo right down his brother's shoulder and arm. That was a good day. Maybe today it would happen again. He hoped so.

After washing himself beside the tank, Pascal got dressed, then opened the gate to Iggy's pen, slipped her halter around her neck and led her outside. "Come on, you're over here today," he said, heading for the opposite side of the garden from the Malolos'. On the way he stopped to yank a long metal pole out of the ground, which he drove back into the soft soil when he got closer to the fence. He slipped the loop at the loose end of the halter over the end of the pole, then went to find a heavy stick or something that he could use to knock the pole just a little farther into the ground.

"There," he said when he'd hammered the pole in. "I'll get your water tub and then you'll be set for the day."

Going to the same hole in the fence that he'd stood at the day before. Peering into the Malolos' yard.

A single chicken pecking around the garden beds. The door of the chicken shed wide open. The goat pen empty, the halter lying on the ground in front of the open gate. No sign of the Malolos' goat.

No sign of the rest of the Malolos' chickens.

No sign of the Malolos.

An empty house, an empty yard.

The school was small, maybe sixty or seventy children. In about half a year, Jean-Baptiste would be going to the secondary school in Ruhengeri. But for now, he was one of the big kids who sat at the back of the classroom and picked on the little ones when Miss Uwazuba wasn't paying attention. This happened quite a lot, since she was in love.

She'd told them on the first day of the year. "Children, I hope you'll forgive me if I seem a little distracted," she'd said. "It's a reason that you might not completely understand, but I'll tell you anyway. I'm in love."

The smallest children looked puzzled or confused when she said this. The eldest kids, like Jean-Baptiste and that snake Kami, all made kissing noises, or went, "Oooh, Miss is in love!" and slapped each other on the backs. But those in the middle grades — kids like Pascal and his friends — giggled and glanced at each other with embarrassed looks. And Pascal had felt just a little bit sad. He liked Miss Uwazuba. A lot. Her name meant "sun," and that was how she made him feel. Like someone had drawn back curtains in a dark room.

But when she'd said that she was in love, and began to talk about her boyfriend, a man who worked at the tourist lodge as a gardener and handyman, he'd felt a sadness settle over him. Every day he'd hope that she might tell them all that she was no longer in love. But she never did. He guessed that any day now she'd call everyone into the classroom and announce that she and the gardener were going to get married. And he'd have to accept that she had a life outside school. A life that didn't involve her students, or him, or anyone other than her family, the gardener's family and their friends.

The day was coming. He just knew it.

But it wasn't today, because when Miss Uwazuba rang the small handbell to call everyone into class, her eyes were red, and her gaze was distant.

"Sit down, please," she said. "Quickly." There was no smile today. Today she was more like Miss Ikibunda — in Kinyarwanda, that word meant "dark, cloudy sky."

It was pretty clear that all the kids knew something was wrong. Even those who might ordinarily have tried to say something clever or cheeky said nothing.

"Six- and seven-year-olds, take out the exercise I gave you on Friday. Finish it quickly and quietly."

How odd, thought Pascal. How odd that today, for the very first Monday he could remember, Miss Uwazuba had not asked them about their weekend. Not a mention of church, or what they'd done, whether they'd played games or worked in the gardens with their parents. Nothing. Just instructions to get on with their work.

"Eleven- and twelve-year-olds, last week I gave you a French worksheet. I'd like you to carry on with that."

Pascal had to ask. "Miss, is everything all right?"

"Who's calling out?" she snapped, without even looking up from the small notepad she was holding. "Was that you, Henri?"

"No!" Henri said. "No, Miss, it was ... someone else."

"Who, then? Who?"

"Um ... " Henri said, stalling. Staring at the desk, glancing sideways at Pascal.

"Henri?" Miss Uwazuba asked again.

"It was me," Pascal admitted.

"And what did you ask me?"

"I asked if you were all right."

Miss Uwazuba scowled at him. "Why would you ask your teacher such a question, Pascal? That's not any of your business, is it?"

"No, Miss," he said. "I'm sorry, Miss."

"See me during the morning break, Pascal."

"Yes, Miss." It looked like he was in trouble, and he hadn't even found out what was wrong with Miss Uwazuba.

But something definitely was.

Morning break. When everyone stood up to leave the classroom, Pascal stood as well. But he didn't leave. He waited back. Ready for trouble to arrive. Ready for Miss Uwazuba.

Henri patted him on the back. "It's been nice knowing you," he said as he left. "Paul, wait for me!"

Pascal decided to get in quickly, before Miss Uwazuba had a chance to get too angry. "Miss," he said. "I'm sorry I called out. And I'm sorry I asked you about something that wasn't my business."

"Thank you, Pascal. I expect better from you. You're one of my best students."

"Yes, Miss."

"Your parents would be very disappointed."

He stared at the floor. "I know. I'm sorry, Miss."

He still wanted to ask, though. He wanted to ask again. But he couldn't. How could he apologize for asking about something that wasn't his business, then say, "But seriously, what's wrong?"

In the end, he did something slightly different. But almost the same.

"Miss, I only asked if you were okay because you looked sad. You looked sad, and I hoped you were all right. That's all. I'm sorry."

As if she'd just heard the worst news possible, she sat down on the end of one of the benches that ran along behind the desks. Blowing out a long, sighing breath: "Pascal, thank you for worrying, but there's nothing you can do. There's nothing anyone can do. It's all just awful."

Pascal was suddenly aware of how awkward he must have appeared at that moment, standing there in the middle of the classroom with nothing much to say while his teacher sat behind a desk looking like she was about to cry.

"Miss . . ."

"No, it's all too awful for words, Pascal. What a world this is. Most people just want to be in love, want to be happy. Want to make a life for themselves. And some can. If they're born right, if you know what I mean."

He wasn't sure what she meant at all. Born right? He

thought about Father Oscar's hand, like a bird's claw. Was that what she meant? Had *he* been born wrong?

"Miss . . ."

"Thank you for asking if I was all right, Pascal. I will be. Now go and play. I'll be ringing the bell soon."

"Yes, Miss."

As Pascal reached the door, he looked back.

Miss Uwazuba was still sitting at the desk, but she was staring out the window. He was sure he saw the dampness of tears on her cheek.

Maybe he was getting what he'd always hoped for. So why didn't it feel like something he could be happy about?

Tuesday 16 March 1999

She and her boyfriend had broken up, hadn't they?

Kind of, but it was worse than that.

Oh, really? He'd died?

No. But it probably would have been better if he had. In the long run, I mean.

That's quite a dramatic thing to say.

Well, it's true. Actually, it might have been better if they'd never met at all. They were kind of like . . . Who are those kids who fall in love in that play?

Romeo and Juliet?

Yes, that's them. A Hutu Romeo and a Tutsi Juliet.

Can you tell me a little more about the Hutu and the Tutsi? One group was in charge, but there were only a few of them, and the other group was . . . there were lots more of them, but they felt like they didn't have any power.

Do you know which was which?

I think the Hutu were the ones who . . . No, I'm not sure, to be honest. I do know that what happened next was terrible, and the whole world sat by and watched.

Did nothing.

Yes. Did nothing. Which was terrible.

That's one word for it.

What word would you use?

I don't think there are any words.

No. No . . . Well, Pascal, I'm sorry to have to stop now, but I think I just heard the end-of-lunch bell. Will I see you tomorrow?

I don't know. Will you?

Yes, I do want to see you tomorrow. Same time?

I guess. If you say so.

I do. Bye, Pascal.

Collège Secondaire de Saint Matthieu, Belgium

Wednesday 17 March 1999

Good afternoon, Pascal. How are you today?

I don't know. Fine. Look, how much longer are we going to have to do this?

You don't think it's useful?

Do you?

It's helping me understand why you've been behaving the way you have.

And why is that? What's it called? Does it have a name?

I don't think it's helpful to start using labels.

Why not? That's what you guys do, isn't it? Give names to things, then try to fix them?

Sort of. Not really, but yes, in a way.

That doesn't make any sense.

It doesn't? I'm sorry about that. Hopefully by the end of our time together it'll make more sense.

Okay.

So where were we? You'd just been talking to your teacher, Miss ...?

Miss Uwazuba.

Right. And she was sad about something. Her boyfriend, I think? They'd broken up because of the tension between the Hutu and the Tutsi?

Yes.

Did you know at the time?

No. Hey, can I ask you one more thing?

Of course.

This is turning into a story, isn't it?

A story?

I mean, I started talking about my church and the bell and my brother ringing it, and now here we are talking about what happened a few days later. If you want me to, I can just go straight to the part where the guys with the machetes and clubs came along in their trucks and started —

No.

Why not? I mean, isn't that the bit you're really interested in?

No, I want to hear about all of it — your town and your family and your church and Father Oscar and so on. It helps me understand.

Understand what?

Understand what happened later on.

But that's what I keep telling you. You *can't* understand.

Because I wasn't there?

No! Because none of it made any sense, not even to the people who were there! It made no sense at all — my happy, beautiful teacher, the lady in our back garden, Father Michel, the goat . . .

Are you all right?

You're a bit thick, aren't you? Of course I'm not all right!

Pascal, I'm just trying to understand. *Trying*, I said. Why don't you tell me about Father Michel?

I'd rather talk about Father Oscar.

All right, then. Talk to me about Father Oscar. In your own time.

Agabande, Rwanda

Monday afternoon, after school. Behind the church and beyond the long line of shrubs was the low, pale blue dormitory building where Father Oscar and the other male seminary students lived. Pascal had visited Father Oscar at the seminary many times, chatting to him as he swept the front steps or weeded the little garden under the windows of Father Michel's house.

Father Michel's house. Dark windows for eyes, a hard line of gutter above those eyes, a yawning mouth.

Today, Father Oscar was cleaning out the goat pen, with a small shovel held in his good hand and the handle of an old plastic bucket hooked over the wrist of the crooked one. Pascal had a second bucket, and was pouring water into the goats' drinking trough.

"When you come here to study, this might be your job," Father Oscar said.

"Scraping up goat poo? I don't think so," Pascal replied. "I do that enough at home already."

"Hmm," said Father Oscar.

"Anyway, I haven't decided whether or not I even want to be a priest," Pascal went on. "I think I'm a bit too young to know."

Father Oscar didn't say anything. Instead, he made a little grunting noise of disagreement.

"When did you know?" Pascal asked. "When did you decide to do this?" He waved his hand in the direction of the main seminary buildings, just to make it clear that he didn't mean cleaning out goat pens.

Father Oscar gave a tiny shrug and cleared his throat. "I think . . . I think when I was ten, maybe."

"Ten?"

He nodded. "I don't remember much before that anyway. So I think I always knew. Yes, always."

"You were ten?"

"Serving God."

Pascal waited. There had to be more to come. "Serving God" wasn't even a proper sentence.

"It's all I ever wanted to do," Father Oscar finished.

"But you're not serving God," Pascal said. "Not today."

There was a sudden flash of anger in the young priest's eyes, a flash the colour of bruised pride. "No? So what should I be doing instead? Tell me."

Pascal shrugged. "I don't know — priest stuff, I guess. Communion, or confession. Or looking after sick people, like the nuns do. But not . . . not *this*. Not cleaning out goat pens."

Father Oscar's gaze was steady, and a little frightening. He didn't say anything for a long time, but Pascal found it impossible to look away. Bruised, proud anger.

"The thirteenth chapter of the Gospel of John," Father Oscar said at last. "Do you remember it?"

Pascal shook his head dumbly. He didn't know the

chapters of the Bible by number yet.

"Jesus washing the disciples' feet. Remember this story?"

Now Pascal nodded. "I do, I just didn't know —"

"Do you know why Jesus did that?"

"Um . . ."

"He did it because his disciples' feet were dusty. It's very dry over there in the Holy Land. After a long day of walking, it was good to wash off all the dust. If you had guests, that's what you did. The first thing. Get the dust off their feet."

"I don't —"

"Usually your servant would do that job."

"But Jesus wasn't a servant," Pascal said. "He was the boss of the disciples. They were following *him*, not the other way around."

"Yes."

There was another pause. A long pause. Father Oscar still staring.

"So . . ."

Now, at long last, Father Oscar's face relaxed into a smile. "Yet Jesus still washed their feet. So if Jesus was humble enough to wash his disciples' feet like a servant, I think I can be humble enough to muck the poo out of his goat shed. Do you see?"

Pascal nodded. He understood and felt stupid, both at the same time.

"I'm sorry," he said.

Father Oscar handed him the filthy bucket and winked. "Throw this on the garden and everything will be forgiven."

"No need for confession?" Pascal asked.

"No, just the poo on the garden."

As Pascal carried the bucket out of the goat yard and turned to close the crooked gate behind him, he sensed that he was being watched. Then, when he looked around, he saw that he was right. Father Michel was standing at the back corner of the church, his hands clasped together in front of him, his long white cassock hanging down almost to the ground.

"Good afternoon, Father," Pascal called.

Father Michel didn't say anything. He simply stared a little longer, gave a very small nod and turned away, walking around the end of the church and out of sight.

"I think he's weird," Pascal whispered, staring into the blackness above him.

"He *is* weird," Jean-Baptiste whispered back. "I don't like him. That's why I didn't volunteer to be an altar boy. I don't think he likes kids very much."

"I don't think he likes *anyone* very much," Pascal replied. "Even when he shakes hands with everyone after Mass he doesn't smile or anything. Why did he even become a priest if he doesn't like people?"

"I bet I know why," Jean-Baptiste whispered. "I bet he likes hearing people confess stuff to him."

"What sort of things do you think they confess?"

"Bad stuff. Stealing stuff. Being mean to kids or animals. Using swear words."

"Telling lies?"

"Oh, definitely. Telling lies would be one of the main ones."

"What about killing someone?"

"That one doesn't happen very often."

"I know, but if it did, would that be something the bad person would confess to Father Michel?"

"I guess so. I mean, that's one of the Ten Commandments, isn't it? I think it's maybe the first one."

Pascal was pretty sure that his brother was wrong. "Thou shalt not kill" was number five, maybe six. But that wasn't important right now. There were bigger questions to think about. "So if someone goes and confesses that they've done something really bad, like beating up an old lady or doing a murder, doesn't Father Michel have to tell the police or the army or someone like that?" he asked.

"No, that's the thing," Jean-Baptiste replied. "That's why confession is so good. He can't tell anyone."

"Anyone at all?"

"*Anyone*. It's called the lawyer-client privilege, I think."

Pascal was pretty sure his brother was wrong about this, too. Wasn't lawyer-client privilege something to do with lawyers and their clients? But it sounded kind of right as well, even if the name was wrong.

"Hey, J-B."

"What?"

"Do you think you'll ever give up ringing the bell?"

Now a third voice joined the conversation. "Maaaama!" Nadine wailed.

"Shut up, squirt!" Jean-Baptiste hissed. "Do you want us to get in trouble?"

"Maaaama! J-B told me to shut up!"

Pascal heard his brother groan. In his head he counted slowly. One . . . two . . . three . . . four . . . five . . .

Right on cue, the door opened a crack. Papa's face was there in the gap, lit from below by his flashlight. "Boys. We've been over this. Sleep, now."

The room darkened as the gap began to close.

"Papa!" Pascal called, in a voice slightly above a whisper, even though everyone in the room was awake now.

The gap widened again. "Yes, son?"

"What do you think of Father Michel?"

Papa didn't answer for a moment.

"Papa?"

"I'm thinking."

Thinking? What was there to think about? Somewhere nearby a dog howled — it was probably Hector, the N'Drandas' big dog — and was answered by the bark of another, much farther away.

"I think Father Michel cares about his country. But I also think he cares about his country maybe a little more than he cares about the people in his church. *Some* of the people."

"So what did he mean yesterday, when he said that we should love our neighbours?" Pascal asked.

"There's a big difference between knowing what you should do and actually doing it," Papa replied. "Now go to sleep — it's late."

The moment the door closed, Nadine whispered, "I told you to be quiet, but you weren't, and now you're in trouble."

"You didn't tell us to be quiet," Jean-Baptiste whispered back. "You just started shouting for Mama, you big baby."

"I'm not a baby! I'm five!"

"Not yet, you're not," Jean-Baptiste replied.

"Well, when I wake up I will be."

"*If* you wake up," Jean-Baptiste whispered.

"Maaaama!"

"Good one," Pascal hissed at Jean-Baptiste.

One . . . two . . . three . . . four . . . five . . .

The door opening. Papa's voice low, cross. "Boys, don't make me come back here a third time."

"J-B said he was going to kill me!" Nadine wailed.

"Jean-Baptiste!"

"I didn't, Papa, I promise!"

"He didn't," Pascal said. His brother annoyed him more than anyone should ever annoy another person, but this was the truth. And truth had to be defended. Even if it was going to help the boy who never missed a chance to wake him up in the most horrible way.

"We don't talk about killing people in this house," Papa said sternly.

"But I didn't!" Jean-Baptiste protested again.

"He really didn't," Pascal said.

"All right. Whatever was said, do *not* make me come back to this room again. Am I clear?"

"Yes, Papa," the boys answered.

Nadine said nothing.

"Good night." Papa closed the door quietly, and once again Hector the dog howled. Once again the faraway dog barked.

Then came silence.

Tuesday 5 April 1994

The next morning was the same as every other, with one major difference. It was Nadine's fifth birthday.

And that meant that she was more annoying than usual.

She bounced in front of the boys as they walked through the kitchen on their way to the backyard. "Guess what, J-B! Guess what, Scally! It's my birthday!"

"Congratulations," Jean-Baptiste said. "Out of my way."

Nadine wasn't put off. "I'm this many!" Holding up three fingers on one hand, four on the other.

"Close," Mama said, smiling at the boys from behind Nadine. "Five is big, isn't it, boys?" Opening her eyes wide, practically pleading with them to show a bit more excitement.

"Pretty big," Pascal agreed, still trying to get the water out of his ear. Water that his revolting brother had dribbled in there while Pascal was still asleep.

Nadine wasn't finished. "And guess what else!" A command, not a question.

"No," Jean-Baptiste replied, pushing past his little sister. "Out of the way — I've got a cow to milk."

"What else?" Pascal asked her. Of course she could be annoying, but she was still his little sister, and it was still her birthday. It wouldn't kill him to show her a bit of interest.

"I got this!" She held up a doll. It was made from an old sock stuffed with something. Its eyes were buttons, its hair strands of black wool. "His name is Macaron!"

"That's great!" Pascal said.

"And guess what else! I'm having a party," she said. "A birthday party."

"Really?"

"Yeah. Tonight."

Pascal looked at Mama, who nodded. Meanwhile Jean-Baptiste had stopped at the back door, turned long enough to hear this thrilling news, then left.

"I love birthday parties!" Pascal said to Nadine. "Am I invited?"

His sister giggled. "Of course not! You're a boy!"

"Never mind," he said. Then, because his brother wasn't there to see him do it, he bent down and kissed Nadine on the cheek.

She wiped it off straight away. "*Bleuch!* I'm not Iggy!"

Walking past Lucé's stall, hearing Jean-Baptiste muttering something under his breath. "What's wrong with you?" Already knowing, but asking anyway.

"A birthday party. I've never had one of those. How come that little cockroach gets one?"

"I don't think you should use that word."

"Why not? That's what she is."

"Papa says —"

"Papa says! Papa says! So what? Anyway, she's having a party, and I've never had one."

Pascal knew this wasn't true. He remembered a couple of years earlier, when Jean-Baptiste turned ten. Potato chips and Fanta. Only a small packet of chips, only a small bottle of Fanta, and everyone had got little more than a taste of each. But they'd sung a song, and Papa had said a prayer for his son, and they'd had some lovely food. Probably cassava stew, and *isombe*, maybe with some *matoke* as well. Plus the chips and Fanta, just as a special birthday treat.

But Pascal didn't correct his brother. What was the point?

He went over to the fence, and the hole to next door. He looked through. No chickens, no goat, no Malolos, no sign of life. But someone had been there. Someone had been there with a knife or a machete of some kind, because all of the Malolos' banana trees had been slashed to the ground. The tall ones with almost-ready bunches of fruit, the suckers, all of them. They'd been hit with one stroke through the soft, pulpy trunks, then more, and more, until the trunks were like a mush of purple and green and yellow.

And the bunches of bananas, still green, also slashed and ruined. They had been doomed the moment the trunks were cut, but then whoever had done this had seen the need to stay a little longer and to completely destroy bunches that could never ripen now anyway.

Looking closer. Other destruction. Cassava plants cut off almost at ground level, the thin trunks slashed into short, uneven lengths. Bean plants torn from the ground and thrown to one side.

And the chicken pen kicked open, smashed, the poles

that kept the hens safe at night hacked or kicked until they were jagged and splintered.

And across the whitewashed wall at the back of the house some word was scrawled. Pascal couldn't read it. A small part of him knew that it was probably best that way.

A window was smashed.

The animals were all gone, and Pascal was glad. Something told him that if the animals had still been there, they might not have survived the terrible machetes that someone had wielded around that garden. Swung around madly amongst those plants and crops and trees.

"Pascal. What are you doing?" His brother was standing behind him, holding the milk bucket. "What are you doing?" he asked again when Pascal didn't reply immediately.

"Come here. Look at this."

"At what? I've got to get ready for school, and we haven't eaten yet."

"I know. But come here first. It'll only take a second."

Jean-Baptiste placed the bucket on the ground and came across. "What?"

"Look through there." Pointing at the hole in the fence.

Jean-Baptiste looking through the hole. Frowning, unsure of what he was meant to be looking at. "I don't . . ."

"See the garden? It's been all cut down and pulled out."

"Who did that?"

"I don't know."

"Where are the Malolos?"

"I don't know. I told you the other day, they said they were leaving."

"And they ruined their garden before they went? That doesn't make any sense."

"I know," said Pascal. "That's why I showed you."

"Boys?" Mama calling from the back door. Standing there, holding the door open with one hand, the other hand resting on her hip. "Come away now, boys."

"But Mama . . ." Jean-Baptiste replied.

"Now. Which means immediately. No talking back."

Letting the passion fruit vine fall back over the hole in the fence, Pascal started to walk towards Mama. Jean-Baptiste seemed a little less willing to do as he was told, but he also knew better than to argue. That was why he hesitated, just for a moment, before sighing, picking up the milk bucket and following Pascal.

"Mama, they're gone, just like I told you," Pascal said. "And all their animals are gone, too. And someone —"

"Just come inside," Mama said, shepherding the boys into the house. "Wait, Pascal — have you done your morning chores yet? The chickens? The goat?"

"No, Mama. I got distracted."

Mama cuffed him gently on the back of his head. "Go on, get out there, and do it quickly. And come straight back in, do you hear me? No dawdling around. School starts soon, and you don't want to be late. Oh, and I need you to come straight home after school today."

"Why?" Pascal asked.

"I might need your help to set up your sister's birthday party."

"Why can't she help? Or Jean-Baptiste?"

This time there was no cuff to the back of the head. There was just a stern glare. "Chores, school, straight home, do you hear me? No going home with Henri after school."

"Yes, Mama," Pascal agreed.

Pascal wouldn't have been able to go home with Henri after school even if he'd wanted to. That was because Henri wasn't at school.

If Miss Uwazuba noticed, she didn't let on. She just did what she normally did — tried to manage a classroom of more than fifty students without losing her temper.

Today, she wasn't doing that last part very well. She was sad one minute, cranky the next, and even told Jean-Baptiste and Kami to shut up, which she never did.

But Pascal didn't even *think* about asking if she was okay. He didn't need to. It was completely obvious that she wasn't.

In the end, she told everyone not to come back from lunch. "Just go home," she said. "Apologize to your parents, but I can't do this today. I have a lot on my mind. And that means I'm not teaching very well."

The kids all looked around at one another. This had never happened before.

"So go," Miss Uwazuba said, waving her hands at them. "What do you want — a written invitation? Go!"

They didn't need to be told a third time.

At home, things weren't much better than they'd been at school. That was because Mama was in a flap.

That sometimes happened, and it was never much fun. Pascal was fairly sure that Jean-Baptiste enjoyed it.

Sometimes he'd actually try to annoy Mama, as if needling her was the joke, and getting her to explode was the punchline.

But not Pascal. He wasn't even slightly interested in making Mama so much as grumble, let alone explode. He liked it just fine when she was singing quietly to herself. Or shouting at his brother.

But this time she wasn't in a flap because of something Jean-Baptiste had done to irritate her. This time she was in a flap because Nadine was having her fifth birthday party that night.

"What are you doing home?" she asked the boys as they came in. "Is school over? What time is it?"

"Miss sent us home early," Jean-Baptiste answered. "She was . . . I don't know what the word is."

"She was crying and cross and kept forgetting what she'd just said," Pascal explained. "So in the end she just said, 'Get out of here.'"

"Hmm," said Mama. "Well, in that case I've got some extra jobs for you to do in the garden and around the house. Pascal, where's your brother? He was here a second ago!"

Pascal shrugged. Over the years, Jean-Baptiste had managed to refine the art of disappearing at just the right time.

"Oh well. In that case, I've got a job for you," she said, and Pascal sighed. Quietly, and mostly inside. This was how it usually worked — Mama had extra chores, Jean-Baptiste vanished, Pascal was given the task. And there was never any point arguing. Especially not today. Mama's tone made it very clear that she wasn't in the mood.

"Yes, Mama?"

"Here." She handed him a list, her string shopping bag and some paper money. "I need you to go down to Mr. Ingabire's store."

Pascal read the list. Mostly it was the usual kind of things — oil, sugar, flour. But near the end was a surprise.

"Coca-Cola? But we never have Coca-Cola!"

"It's not every day that your sister turns five," Mama replied without looking up. She flapped her hand at him. "Go! And put that money somewhere safe. I don't want you to drop it."

Pascal wondered what was so special about the number five. In the last few years he'd turned six, seven, eight, nine, ten *and* eleven, and he'd never once had Coca-Cola to celebrate. Maybe that was because Nadine was the only girl in the family. That was the way these things usually seemed to work.

"And what's this one?" he asked, trying to read the very last item on the list.

"Pringles."

"The potato chips?" Pascal had seen the bright red cardboard tubes in Mr. Ingabire's store, sitting there on the shelf, proud as anything. He'd often wondered what they tasted like. "Aren't they expensive?"

"Yes, but you should have enough money there for two tubes."

"*Two* tubes?"

"Yes. A red one and a green one. Your sister's having two friends around."

Now this was getting very strange. Pascal didn't know that his sister even had two friends!

"Well?" Mama said. "What are you waiting for? Go!"

"Can I take Henri?"

"To the shop? But he lives all the way over on the other side of the valley! And you've been with him all day!"

Pascal shook his head. "He wasn't at school today."

"Is he ill?"

"I don't know," Pascal admitted. "I should go and see if he's okay, don't you think, Mama? That's what a good friend would do."

Mama pulled a crooked smile.

"I'll run," Pascal promised. "It won't take very much longer."

"All right. But no dawdling. Mr. Ingabire always closes right on time."

"I know," Pascal replied. "I'll be quick."

"Oh, and there's one more thing," Mama said as he got to the front door. "M&Ms. A big packet. Or maybe those other American chocolate candies. What are they called?"

"Do you mean Hershey Kisses?"

"Yes. Something like that. You should have enough money there."

Pascal jogged most of the way down to the town and half the way up the hill on the other side before he had to stop and rub the stitch in his side. By the time he got to Henri's house he was shiny with sweat, and his shirt was sticking to his back.

He knocked on the front door twice, but no one

answered, so he went around the end of the house, being careful not to step in any of the little surprises Henri's dogs had left in the grass.

When he reached the window of the room that Henri shared with his father, he pulled himself up onto the sill and propped there on his elbows.

Henri was inside, sitting cross-legged on his bed with his tractor, which now had the wire steering wheel secured to it. He was working intently at one of the wooden wheels with his pocket knife.

"What are you doing?" Pascal asked, and Henri looked around a couple of times before realizing that the voice had come from the open window.

"Hey!"

Pascal clambered in through the window and sat down on the other bed. "What's wrong with your tractor?"

"Nothing. I'm just carving some tread into the wheels. You know, like real tires. So it leaves a proper track in the dirt."

"Oh, that's a good idea," Pascal said. "Can I do that with mine?"

Henri shrugged. "Sure. Do whatever you like. So, I didn't know you were coming over."

"I'm not staying long. I just came to ask if you wanted to come to the shop with me."

Henri frowned at him. "Why?"

"Just for fun. I've got to buy all this stuff for Nadine's party. We can get a shaved ice."

Henri closed his eyes and sighed. "Shaved ice . . . That

does sound good." He opened one eye. "But I don't have any money."

"I've got heaps," Pascal said, taking the paper money out of his pocket.

Henri's eyes widened. He put down his knife and reached out his hand, but Pascal pulled the money away.

"Where did you get all that?" Henri asked.

"From Mama. I told you, I'm buying supplies for Nadine's party."

"What sort of party? Is she getting married?"

Pascal laughed. "No, she's turning five. Mama thinks Nadine won't love her any more if she doesn't have Pringles and M&Ms and Coca-Cola."

"I love Coke," Henri sighed. "I haven't had it forever."

"So, shaved ice?" Pascal asked.

Henri pursed his lips and thought. "Okay. But then I have to come straight home."

They hurried down the hill towards town, cutting down through the cassava plantation and plantain trees behind Henri's house. Pascal was so excited, not because of the shaved ice, even though that thought was quite exciting, but because of the large amount of money he was carrying in his pocket. His friend was going to see him spending it, and after all, what was the point of having an important amount of money in your pocket if no one got to see you spending it?

It was starting to rain. It was like this most afternoons during the wet season. It would probably stop soon, but even if it didn't, it wouldn't matter. It was just water.

"Good for our tank," Pascal said.

"I wish we had a tank," Henri replied.

"You should get one."

"That's what I said to Dad. I said, 'We should get a water tank like Pascal's family.'" But he got all cranky, and said it was all right for you, with your big brother working in Belgium and your dad having a government job in Ruhengeri, up in your fancy . . ."

"Our fancy what?"

"It doesn't matter."

"Our fancy what?"

"Your house."

"You've got a house too."

"Yes, I know, but . . . Never mind."

For a moment, the idea of spending money in front of his friend felt less exciting.

But Pascal knew that feeling wouldn't last.

They reached the bottom of the hill and waited for some traffic to go past on the main road. It wasn't much — a small truck, a van, a beaten-up taxi, some scooters and some bikes. Pretty much a regular afternoon in Agabande.

Out in front of his shop, Mr. Ingabire was talking to two men. He was standing in the doorway, holding his broom of course, and the other men were on either side of the door. Pascal didn't recognize the man standing on the left, but the other one crouched down on the opposite side he did remember. Clement, with the knotty walking stick. The other man seemed to be grinning, except it wasn't a happy grin. His mouth was twisted upwards in more of a sneer than a smile. Something about him made Pascal feel very uncomfortable. Perhaps it was the long machete he was cradling between his knees.

Finally there was a gap in the traffic, and the boys crossed the street.

"Hello, boys," Mr. Ingabire said as they reached the store. He scowled at their bare feet. "I just finished sweeping, you know. Now it'll need to be done all over again."

"We'll make sure we do it properly this time," Smiley-man said. "Completely. So it never needs to be done again, ever."

Clement chuckled, but Mr. Ingabire threw Smiley-man a warning look. "Not now," he said.

Smiley-man grunted. "Maybe not now, but very soon. Very soon. Come on," he said to Clement as he straightened and stood. "Just remember, cleaning day is coming. Make sure you're ready."

"That's right," Clement agreed. "No room in the middle. One or the other. You'll have to choose."

They began to stroll away, in no hurry at all, and as they went past Pascal and Henri, Pascal heard one of them mutter something.

"Psst," Mr. Ingabire hissed, like a cornered cat.

"Cleaning day," Smiley-man said, turning his head to stare deep into Pascal's eyes. Then the two men walked off down the middle of the road, with Smiley-man dragging the tip of his machete along the asphalt. It made an awful metallic scratching sound that rang out around the crooked houses and buildings of the town, and threatened to drown out the sound of the cars, vans and motorbikes.

"Come on in, boys," Mr. Ingabire said. He didn't seem concerned about the dirt any more. Instead he glanced up and down the street a couple of times before herding them into his shop.

"Mr. Ingabire, who were those men?" Henri asked.

Mr. Ingabire lifted the flap at the end of the counter and took his place in front of all the shelves. "They were no one important."

"I think one of them works with my dad," Henri said.

"It's possible. I wouldn't really know. Now, what can I get you?"

Pascal took out the list and placed it on the counter for Mr. Ingabire to read. Next to it he put the shopping bag.

"Pringles?" Mr. Ingabire said when he reached the end of the list.

"Two packets." Pascal checked the shelf and saw three tubes of Pringles, all of them red. "They're for Nadine's birthday. My little sister. She's turning five."

"Is she? I remember when she was born. I remember when *you* were born, Pascal. You were very small. Your parents weren't sure if you'd even survive."

"But I did."

"Yes, you did. You were a fighter. That's what your father told me. He said, 'Mr. Ingabire, I have another son, and even though he's very small, I know he'll survive, because he is a fighter.'"

Pascal grinned and flexed his muscles.

"So, Coca-Cola and Pringles." Mr. Ingabire reached up, took two of the red tubes and placed them into the string bag with the other groceries. From a lower shelf he grabbed a large bottle of Coke, and that went in the bag as well. He took the pencil from behind his ear and began to write down the prices on a scrap of paper, ready to add them up.

"Oh, I nearly forgot!" Pascal said. "And M&Ms!"

Mr. Ingabire stared at him. "American chocolate too? Wow, this is going to be some party, isn't it?" He turned to the small rack of candy and chocolates at the end of the counter and took out a packet of M&Ms, which also went in the bag. He poised the pencil above the paper. "Anything else?"

Pascal looked at the money in his hand. Was it going to be enough to buy all of that, as well as a couple of shaved ices? Mama would be expecting change.

"No, that's all," he said, handing over the money.

Henri poked him in the ribs.

"Quit it!"

"But the shaved ices . . . !"

"Sorry. But I don't think I have enough."

"You shouldn't have promised."

"Do you want them or not?" Mr. Ingabire asked, still holding the change.

"I don't know if I have enough," Pascal said.

Mr. Ingabire opened his hand, looked at the money in his palm. There wasn't much there — only a couple of coins. "Two shaved ices? Nope, not enough here. Sorry, boys." He held out his hand, and Pascal took back the coins from him.

"Never mind. Sorry, Henri," Pascal said.

"You promised," Henri replied. Sulking.

Mr. Ingabire took a deep breath. "Wait right there," he said, before going out through the little door behind the counter. He returned a few seconds later with two shaved ices, which he gave to the boys.

"Thank you!" the boys said together.

Mr. Ingabire handed the bag of groceries to Pascal. "Go on, get out of here with those things before they melt and make my clean floor all sticky."

"You know what I've been thinking?" Pascal said as he and Henri stood out the front of Mr. Ingabire's store, their shaved ices disappearing fast. Some down their throats, a lot down their arms.

"I can't think anything," Henri said, his face twisting and contorting. "My brain is freezing! Why does this happen when you eat something cold?"

"Well, what *I've* been thinking about is how unfair it is that my sister gets two tubes of Pringles, a big bottle of Coca-Cola *and* M&Ms."

"She's a lucky girl," Henri agreed. "But you'll get to have some, won't you? She'll share, right?"

"Probably not. You know what sisters are like."

"But you will get some party food, won't you?"

"Nadine's going to be all bossy. She'll be showing off to her friends, and she'll say, 'These aren't for you, Scally! Get out!' And Mama will send me into the other room."

"Hmm," Henri replied. "Well, you could just come over to my place."

"Do you have Coke and M&Ms at your place?"

"No, of course not."

"In that case . . . Anyway, I'd better get going. If I take too long she'll make me skip the party altogether, and then there'll be no M&Ms or Coke at all for me."

"Well, I guess I'll see you later," Henri said. "Enjoy the party."

A sudden brilliant idea. "Wait! Do you think Mama would mind if . . ."

"If what?"

Pascal took the brown bag of M&Ms from amongst the other groceries and shook it. The chocolates rattled inside the plastic pack. "Do you think Mama would mind?"

"If you opened them? Of course she would!"

"We wouldn't eat them all."

"No, but . . ."

"We'd only have a few. Maybe . . . five each. No, ten. Eight. Eight each. What do you think?"

Henri shook his head. "She'd definitely notice."

"Just a few. I'll promise not to have any at Nadine's birthday party. I'd tell her that I was just having my share early."

"Do you think she'd be okay with that?"

"Sure," Pascal said. "She'd be fine." Trying to convince himself, but not succeeding.

"Yeah, I don't know . . ." Henri began.

No. Before his friend could make any kind of sense, or put any more doubt in his mind, Pascal had to act. He gripped the top of the packet and pulled it apart.

Oh boy. He knew it had been a mistake immediately.

"Well, I guess it's too late to go back now," he said as

they peered down into the open packet. So many colours. So many delicious colours.

"They do look amazing," Henri sighed. He inhaled deeply.

"Remember, eight each," Pascal said.

"So should we have two of each colour, just so we get to taste them all?" Henri suggested.

"I guess so." Pascal reached into the bag and lifted out a handful of M&Ms. "Put out your hand. Okay, two yellow, two brown, two green, two red, two orange, two tan . . ."

"That's more than eight," Henri said. "That's twelve."

"Hmm. Twelve's not *that many* more than eight."

"I don't even know if they have different flavours."

"I think they do," Pascal said. He popped a red one into his mouth and chewed it slowly. The crisp shell cracked between his back teeth, then the soft, velvety chocolate spread through his mouth. It was good. So, *so* good.

Yellow next. Crisp crack of the shell, then soft velvet. Just as good as the red one. Better? No, not really. Different? Hard to say.

"Well?" Henri asked.

"I don't know. I *think* they're different, but I'm not sure. You try."

"Which one should I try? Orange. I'll try orange."

Henri placed an orange M&M on his tongue and closed his mouth slowly. He shut his eyes as he sucked on the chocolate. "So good," he said.

"Green next," said Pascal. "I'll try a green one as well."

Crisp crack of shell, soft velvet of chocolate. Different? Better? The same? Hard to know.

"What do you think?"

Henri grinned. Chocolate was stuck to his front teeth. "I don't care," he said.

They each tried to make their twelve M&Ms last as long as they could, but far too soon they were gone. All that was left were some smudges of colour on their palms and chocolate on their teeth.

Pascal peered into the bag again. The level still looked pretty high.

Not quite as high as it had looked before they'd eaten twenty-four of them, but still pretty high. Probably enough for them to have a few more. Just a few.

"One more of each of the colours?" he suggested. "Do you think Mama will notice?"

"Of course she's going to notice," Henri said. "You've opened the bag."

"You're right. I don't think one more of each colour will make much of a difference. It's just six more."

"Each. It's six more *each*. That's twelve."

"That's fine," Pascal said. "There'll be heaps left."

They sifted through the M&Ms until they had two of each colour. Then they divided them and ate them slowly.

"They're all the same flavour," Henri said when they'd finished.

"Definitely," Pascal answered. "Which means that we don't need to worry about the colours now."

"What do you mean?"

"Let's just have a few more. But we won't worry about the colours."

"Are you sure?" Henri pulled the top of the bag wider and looked inside.

"Just a few more. There's still heaps," Pascal said. "Hold out your hand."

"There's not many left," Henri said a while later. He picked up the M&Ms packet and shook it. It sounded very empty.

Pascal took the bag and looked inside. Henri was right — only a few of the colourful little chocolates remained.

"She'll definitely notice now," Henri said.

"You're right. We can't hide this."

Henri cleared his throat. "No, *you* can't hide this. I'm not going to be there."

"Well, I can't take this packet home, can I? Not when it's almost empty."

"So what are you going to do?"

"Finish them off, I guess," Pascal said.

"Won't she ask where they are? They were on the list!"

"I'll think of something," Pascal said as he poured the last of the M&Ms into his hand.

But he didn't have even the slightest idea what that something might be.

"You took forever!" Mama said, flicking the radio off as Pascal entered the kitchen. "Where were you?"

"I went and got Henri first. He came with me to the shop."

"I'm in a hurry! I needed the shopping ages ago. I told you that! Here, give it to me."

She snatched the string bag from him and began to place the items on the little kitchen table, one at a time. Maybe it was good that she was a bit cross, Pascal thought. She might not notice that there were no M&Ms. He began to edge towards the door.

"Where are the chocolates?"

"The what?" he asked. Buying time. Even though he'd had the whole walk home to think of a better answer than that.

"The chocolates. The M&Ms. Where are they?"

"Mr. Ingabire didn't have any."

A lie. A terrible lie. But in the circumstances, still probably better than the truth.

"He had no M&Ms?"

"All out."

"Those kiss things?"

"No, none of those either."

"Come here," Mama said. Her finger beckoning. "Come back here." Her finger now pointing at a spot on the floor directly in front of her. This was serious.

"Yes, Mama?"

"Are you stupid?"

"I don't think so."

A liar, maybe, but not stupid, he thought.

"So if you're not stupid, why didn't you think to get some other kind of candy? Didn't he have anything else?"

"I don't know," Pascal answered, quite truthfully. "I wasn't looking to see what other chocolates he had."

"You know what to do," she said. "Your sister can't have a birthday party without candy."

"But you've already got her Pringles and Coca —"

"Go now. I guess you still have some money, if you didn't get any chocolates."

"Yes, Mama," he replied, praying that she wouldn't ask to see it.

"Then go. And hurry. Don't take so long this time. And don't go and get Henri again — there's no time. Straight there and straight back, do you understand?"

"Yes, Mama."

He set out at a jog. Quickly there, quickly back. But by the time he reached the bottom of the shortcut through the dark trees and deep green shadows and was within sight of Mr. Ingabire's shop, he'd slowed to a walk. It was partly the sick, heavy-headed feeling from too much chocolate. But it was more than that. He'd hoped to sneak the change from the first trip back into the money jar before Mama had a chance to count it. But now that they'd talked about it, now that a scene had been made, she'd want to see the change. She'd want to count it. And there wouldn't be enough. She'd know. Whatever he bought to replace the M&Ms, she'd want to know how much they'd cost.

It was going to take something pretty special to get out of this one.

From where Pascal stood in the shadow of the big strangler fig tree, he could see Mr. Ingabire sweeping his front step. Again! Always sweeping.

Chocolate. He had to get chocolate, and he knew what he was going to have to do.

The Sunday School lesson from a few weeks earlier came flooding back to him. Stealing. No stealing. "Thou shalt not steal." Sister Lourdes had said that it was one of the important ones, one of the Ten Commandments. It came right after honouring your parents, not killing and not doing adultery, whatever *that* was. But no matter what doing adultery was, not telling lies came straight after it. He didn't think he was going to be doing any adultering, and he wasn't planning on killing anyone, but so far he'd lied, and it was to his mother. *Lying*, to your *mother* — that was two commandments ticked off in one go!

Two women approached the shop. Mr. Ingabire greeted them, followed them inside.

And Pascal made his move.

His heart racing. Those sweet, velvety M&Ms had turned into a heavy rock in the pit of his stomach. And his hands were shaky — was that something American chocolates could cause?

He still didn't know how he was going to do it. But he knew that it had to be done. He had to at least try.

The women were still in the shop when Pascal walked in. Mr. Ingabire was putting their groceries into their bags. He looked up as Pascal came through the door.

"Oh, you're back."

"Yes. Me again." Smiling, trying to act casual.

"Did you forget something?"

"Kind of."

"Well, give me a minute," Mr. Ingabire said. "I'll just finish serving these lovely ladies."

Checking that there were Hershey Kisses on the rack at the end of the counter. Two packets. One would be enough.

Mr. Ingabire and the women chatted for much longer than they needed to, Pascal thought. The longer they talked, the more anxious he became. The more he imagined his plan going horribly wrong. The plan that seemed worse the longer he stood there listening to the adults having their pointless conversation.

Maybe it would be easier to just admit to Mama that he and Henri had eaten a couple of the M&Ms and couldn't stop. She'd been a kid once. She'd understand. Wouldn't she?

"It can't go on much longer," Mr. Ingabire was saying. "Everyone I talk to has had enough."

"But what will happen?" one of the women replied.

Mr. Ingabire replied by making a kind of squelching noise in his cheek.

"Who? Which ones?"

"All of them, they keep saying."

"*All* of them?"

The other woman turned and looked at Pascal, who was waiting patiently — but less patiently the longer they talked — beside the door. She caught Mr. Ingabire's eye and raised her eyebrows. Just a flicker. A tiny question.

He shook his head. "It's fine," he said. "Don't worry about it. And don't worry about *that*, either. I think most will run off. Burundi, Kenya. Cowards. But I think they'll stay away."

The women left, and Mr. Ingabire straightened his little notepad and returned his stub of pencil to its spot above his ear. "Now, what have you forgotten?"

Mama would understand if he told her the truth. Wouldn't she?

No. No, she wouldn't. It was time for the first lie.

Taking a deep breath in preparation. "I need to buy another shaved ice," he said.

Mr. Ingabire raised his eyebrows. "Really? Two in one day?"

"It's for my brother, Jean-Baptiste. He saw that me and Henri had one, and he was really sad. He even cried. So Mama made me come back down here to get him one."

"I see. Feeling left out, was he?"

"Yeah." Followed by a laugh. A laugh that didn't make a lot of sense. The kind of laugh that could reveal a lie in an instant.

"Well, no one likes to feel left out."

"No."

Pascal knew that the next moment was the most important. If Mr. Ingabire asked him for the money *before* he went to get the shaved ice, the whole plan was ruined. He had to hope he'd go and get it, *then* ask for the money.

"Wait here," Mr. Ingabire said, and he went through the door behind the counter to get the shaved ice.

Now. It had to be now. The first lie had been told; the time for stealing had arrived. Snatching one of the two packets of Hershey Kisses from the candy rack. Lifting the hem of his T-shirt and slipping the Kisses inside the waistband of his shorts. They didn't slide straight in, and he had a brief moment of panic as he fumbled with the packet. But then it was in place, and his shirt was pulled back down.

"Here we go," Mr. Ingabire said as he returned, shaved ice in hand.

One lie complete, stealing done, time for the second lie.

"Oh!" he said, pretending to be surprised. Not sure how well he'd pretended. "I just realized that I left the money at home! Can I pay you next time?"

Mr. Ingabire pointed at a hand-written sign on the front of the counter. *NO CREDIT*. "Pay now, or come back for this later," he said. "Sorry. Rules."

"Oh." Now it was time for Pascal to pretend to be disappointed. "I guess I'll have to tell Jean-Baptiste ... "

"Maybe tell him to stop crying and come and get his own shaved ice next time," Mr. Ingabire suggested.

The strange, nameless sensation in the pit of Pascal's stomach after he left the cool dimness of Mr. Ingabire's shop and returned to the late afternoon light. Partly feeling bad that he had managed to break two of the Ten Commandments in about five minutes. But also feeling excitement at having got away with it.

It wasn't until he was halfway up the shortcut that he took the packet of Hersey Kisses from the waistband of his shorts. And it wasn't until he emerged from the long tunnel of trees at the top of the hill and saw his house that the guilt properly hit him.

And shortly after that the churning sickness in his stomach hit him. The churning sickness that came from eating more chocolate and breaking more commandments in one afternoon than he ever had before.

Getting home. Mama was putting party food on the table in the kitchen. Pascal could hear squeals coming from the kids' bedroom. Squeals of little girls. Nadine and her two friends.

He wanted to ask Mama what time the girls would be going home, but he was frightened to talk to her at all. The fact was, she could see through him. It had always been that way. She could look at his face and instantly know that he'd done something wrong. If he were to speak to her now, it wouldn't be at all surprising if she said, "Son, you've told two lies and stolen something today. Come on — out with it."

He placed the Hershey Kisses on the kitchen bench. "I got them, Mama. Now I've got to go and do my afternoon jobs," he quickly added. And he left as quickly as he'd said it. The less he said, the less chance there'd be that she'd . . .

"Stop."

He stopped. She had him. He'd been so close to escaping. Or so he'd thought.

"Yes, Mama?"

"Don't worry about your afternoon jobs. Jean-Baptiste did them already."

This seemed impossible to believe. Jean-Baptiste doing someone else's work? It was unheard of!

"Why?" he asked.

"Because you had to go back to the shop. So I asked him to help out by doing your jobs for you. Make sure you thank him, won't you?"

"All right," he said. "I will."

And I'll bet he's still going to make sure I never forget it, he thought.

"Now, we're going to eat soon. Can you go and tell Papa that he needs to wash up for dinner?"

"Yes, Mama. Right after I've been to the toilet."

The chocolate was trying to make him suffer.

Pascal really didn't enjoy Nadine's birthday party. There were several reasons. First, it was a birthday party for five-year-olds. Five-year-old *girls*. Silly voices, dumb jokes, not to mention a little sister being rude to her brothers, just to show off to her friends. And a stuffed sock called Macaron being fed party food and drink.

There was a cake. That was all right. It wasn't very big, and it wasn't very fancy, but Mama was proud of it. It even had five candles in the top of it, American-style. They tried singing "Happy Birthday." Then Nadine tried to blow out the candles. She failed — only got three of them to go out. Almost cried. Jean-Baptiste laughed at her, asked how anyone could possibly fail at blowing out candles. That made Nadine cry properly. Mama got cranky, Papa tried not to laugh, even while he was scolding Jean-Baptiste.

There was a taste of Coca-Cola for everyone, but mostly for the birthday girl and her friends. There were enough Pringles for everyone to have a few each, and for the birthday girl and her friends to have lots each. And there were enough Hershey Kisses for everyone to have a couple.

But Pascal didn't. He couldn't.

It wasn't his stomach, overloaded with chocolate. Well,

maybe a bit of that. But mostly it was his mind, overloaded with guilt.

"Mama."

"Yes, son?"

"Can I go to bed?"

She took his face in her hands. Looked into his eyes. Felt his forehead. "Are you all right? Are you sick?"

"No, I'm fine," he said. "I'm just really tired."

"All right. Kiss your sister and wish her a happy birthday before you go."

In bed. Not sleeping. Not even saying his prayers. Why would God want to hear from him, a lying thief?

But then a worse thought came to him. What if he went to sleep but never woke up? There'd be no heaven for him.

Tomorrow. Confession. He would go to the church straight after school and do confession. His life quite possibly depended on it.

Agabande, Rwanda

This morning Pascal wasn't woken by his brother doing something awful to him. He was woken by his mother, gently nudging him awake.

"Pascal. Sleepy-head! Why aren't you out of bed?"

He groaned, rolled over to face the wall. How could he tell his mother about his sleepless night on account of his new life of crime? Two counts of lying and one of theft had left him feeling all churned up.

Mama folded back the mosquito net, felt his forehead. "Are you sick?"

He thought about saying that yes, he was. He'd already made her think he was coming down with something by going to bed early the night before. It would be very easy to let her keep believing that.

Except there was something he had to do. Confession. He'd made it through one night unscathed — he had to confess today. He knew he wouldn't feel better until he had. And he couldn't go and do confession if he spent the whole day at home. You can't be sick one minute and leaving the house to visit the priest the next — not without having to do some pretty fast explaining to your mother.

Now Mama had stopped feeling his forehead, and instead was cupping the nape of his neck. "Pascal?"

"I'm fine, Mama. I'm getting up."

"Are you sure you should? Maybe you should stay in bed."

He pushed her hand away. "Mama! I'm fine, honest. I'll go and do my morning jobs and then I'll run to school."

"Okay," she said. "As long as you're sure. Tell Miss Uwazuba that I said you're to come straight home if you start feeling ill, and I'll take you to Dr. Singh."

A visit to the doctor? If that wasn't going to get him out of bed, nothing would. Last time he'd visited the clinic, Mrs. Singh had given him a needle.

"Am I really late for school?" he asked.

"Not too late to go and do your morning jobs, then wash and get to school," Mama replied as she stood up. "Come on, look busy."

School was shut, the tall gate at the front of the school compound chained and padlocked. Several students were still at the gate, their fingers hooked through the chain-link mesh. It was as if they couldn't think of anything to do.

"Oh, so you made it," Henri said as Pascal walked up. "I thought maybe you ate too much chocolate yesterday."

"Shush!" Pascal hissed, glancing around to make sure that no one had heard. He definitely didn't want Jean-Baptiste to overhear and go telling stories.

His brother wasn't there. Nor were any of his friends. They'd obviously taken the locked gate as a sign that school was not happening today, and they weren't going to hang

118

around long enough to see if it was just some innocent mistake.

But something unwelcome *was* back. The horrible churning in his guts when he was reminded about the M&Ms he and Henri had eaten. And it wasn't the sickness that came from having too much chocolate in his stomach, but the sick feeling that he'd done some terribly, terribly bad thing.

"We should do something," Henri said. "You know, since there's no school today."

Something to take his mind off the confession he knew he was going to have to do later that afternoon. But nothing too dangerous — he didn't want to die before he had a chance to make things right with God.

"Like what?" he asked. "What did you want to do?"

"Ruhengeri," Henri said, simply.

"What do you mean?"

"We could catch the bus to Ruhengeri."

"How?" Pascal asked. "We don't have any money. And the bus costs money."

"That's true," Henri said. "Or we could walk," he suggested brightly.

It wasn't the worst idea ever. Pascal had made the walk maybe four or five times in his life. It was a long way — maybe a couple of hours each direction — but they had nothing better to do.

"What will we do when we get there?" Pascal asked.

Henri shrugged. "I don't know. Walk around, explore ..."

"We have to be back in the afternoon," Pascal said.

"What for?"

How could he explain it to his friend, who didn't even go to church?

"I have to talk to Father Michel," he said. It wasn't a lie. But it didn't say more than it needed to, either.

"Okay," Henri answered. "Let's go. It'll be an adventure!"

"You know what we could do?" Henri said as they stepped off the end of the thin ribbon of asphalt that ran through the town and onto the red clay that would now be the road all the way to Ruhengeri. "We could visit your dad."

"Hmm." Pascal thought about this. He'd never visited his father at work before.

"Do you think he'd mind?" Henri asked.

"Nah. He'll be fine. I'm sure he'd love to see us."

The sound of a horn. Pascal and Henri turned, stepped out of the way as a small truck growled past. In the tray at the back were ten, maybe twelve men, some sitting along the edges, some in the middle.

"Oh, it's Patrick!" Henri said, pointing excitedly. "Hey, Patrick!"

"Who's Patrick?" Pascal asked.

"A friend of my dad's. Hey, Patrick!"

One of the younger-looking men waved from the back of the truck.

"Patrick, give us a ride?" Henri called.

Patrick gave a shrill whistle, and one of the other men thumped on the roof of the cab. The truck stopped, pulled over towards the edge of the road.

"Come on," Henri said, breaking into a jog.

Pascal trotted after him. Strong hands reached down, pulled the boys into the middle of the group of men. Patrick patted Henri on the shoulder.

"Hey, boys, this is Henri. René's kid."

"René's kid!" said one of the other men. "Oh yes, you look just like him. How's your brother? Oliver, is it?"

"He's good," Henri said. "Dad says he's coming home from Kigali soon."

When Henri said this, it was met with a chorus of replies from the other men. Excitement? Approval? It was weird. Hard to tell. But they certainly seemed pleased.

"Tell him we'll save some for him," one of the men said.

Henri looked puzzled. "Save what?"

Some of the men laughed.

"That's the spirit," said one.

"Seriously, save what?" Henri asked.

Patrick rested his hand on the top of Henri's head. "Ask your dad. He'll set you straight. So, who's your friend?"

"I'm Pascal."

"His dad works in Ruhengeri," Henri said. "There's no school today, so we're going to visit him at work."

"He works at the government office," Pascal said. It always made him proud to tell people that. While other people's fathers spent their days working in plantations or gardens, or building roads or houses or fences, his father had an important job. A well-paid job. "He looks after the government trucks and vans and things."

"What, driving them?"

121

"Sometimes."

"What else?"

How to answer? The truth was that he was one of the mechanics who sometimes got to drive the vehicles around town. But that didn't sound all that impressive, to be honest.

"He looks after all the keys," he said. "He decides who gets to borrow the trucks and things. He also looks after the gas."

"Is that right?" Patrick said. "Well, it sounds like he's got a pretty important job."

"Yes, he does," Pascal said. Proud. So proud. Even if it wasn't completely true. The lies were coming more easily.

They were dropped off in the main street of Ruhengeri, in front of a big church, and right across the road from the main government building.

"Take care, boys," Patrick said as they jumped down. "Henri, tell your dad we said hi."

Some of the other men laughed. Weird, thought Pascal— it didn't sound like a joke.

There was a lot more traffic in Ruhengeri than in Agabande. More streets, more shops, more cars, trucks, motorbikes, bicycles, animals, people. More of everything, and it took a lot longer to make their way across the street to the government building than it would have taken to cross the main road back home. Once, Pascal began to cross, but stopped when he noticed that Henri wasn't coming with him. Henri's attention was fixed on a grey-green truck creeping along with the traffic. An army truck.

"Check it out!" Henri was saying. Pointing. "The army!"

"Yeah, I saw it. Come on."

The *BUREAU DES TRAVAUX PUBLICS* — the Office for Public Works — was a large, boxy two-storey building with bars on the windows and a tall gate at the side. Through the gate Pascal could see some of the trucks and vans his father worked on. But he couldn't see Papa anywhere. The boys went up to the gate, hoping to find someone they could ask. Across the yard, Pascal saw a skinny young man using a foot pump to inflate the tire of a small tip-truck. He glanced across, saw the boys outside the gate and kept pumping.

"Excuse me," Pascal called, and finally — reluctantly — the young man left what he was doing and wandered across.

"What?"

"Is my father here?" Pascal asked.

"Who's your father?"

"Moises Turatsinze."

"Oh. Yes. I mean no, he's not here."

"Where is he? Doesn't he work here?"

The young man seemed offended at the question. "I sent him to do an errand."

Pascal glanced at Henri. Had he picked up on that really embarrassing moment, when the young, skinny guy who'd been stamping on a foot pump said that he'd sent Pascal's father on an errand? If Henri had noticed, he didn't let on.

"When will he be back?" Pascal asked.

"I don't know. Soon, I hope. He hasn't got time to mess around, you know. He's got a lot of work to finish before I let him go home."

"I just wanted to say hello," Pascal said. "I wasn't going to stay very —"

"Well, he can't. He's at work. Now get lost before I come out there and teach you a lesson."

"Lionel!" Papa was standing behind the boys, on the footpath. In front of him he held a cardboard box filled with greasy engine parts.

"Oh, Mr. Turatsinze!" the young man said. "I didn't notice you coming back!"

"Yes, I see that," Papa replied. "Get back to work."

"Yes, sir."

"But first, open this gate and take this," Papa said, holding out the box.

"Yes, sir." Lionel did as he was told, took the box. As he turned away, Pascal heard him muttering something beneath his breath.

"Hey!" Without warning, Papa grabbed Pascal's arm and spun him round. "What are you doing here?" he demanded.

"There was no school today. So we came to see you."

"How did you get here?"

"We walked," Pascal told him.

"Only to start with. Then we got picked up," Henri added.

Papa narrowed his eyes. "Picked up? By who?"

"Just some men in a truck," Pascal said.

"'Just some men in a truck?'" Papa frowned. "What are you talking about? Which men, and which truck?"

"It's okay," Henri said. "I knew the men. Or one of them, anyway. His name's Patrick."

"And who is this Patrick?" asked Papa.

"He's a friend of Henri's dad's," Pascal explained.

"Yeah, I know him, so you don't have to get excited," Henri said.

Too far.

The moment it was said, Pascal knew that his friend had gone too far. Talking to Papa that way — it was never going to be let go.

Papa turned slowly towards Henri, his eyes like lumps of dark volcanic rock. "What did you say to me, son?"

Pascal watched his friend's face change. Relaxed one minute, terrified the next. He knew he'd gone too far as well.

"I'm sorry, Mr. Turatsinze," he said, his voice thin and wavering. "I didn't mean to —"

"Here." Papa dug around in his pocket. Glanced around before he pulled out a paper money note. He handed it to Pascal. Kept his eyes on Pascal's. Spoke only to him. "In a few minutes a green bus will stop in front of that telephone pole there. I want you and your rude friend to get on that bus. Buy a ticket each. Do *not* get off that bus until you are in Agabande. Do you understand me?"

"Yes, Papa."

"Mr. Turatsinze . . ." Henri began, but Papa turned to face the gate.

"Go. Both of you. On the bus. No rides in trucks with men. And I expect you to give me some change when I get home, Pascal."

"Yes, Papa."

Wondering if his father knew about the M&Ms and Hershey Kisses.

Wondering how many more things there would be to confess to Father Michel later that day.

For the boys, it was a quiet bus ride home. They'd made it all the way to Ruhengeri, but almost as soon as they arrived, they were on a bus heading straight back to their town.

Neither boy said much. What could they say? To see Papa so angry! Not just with one or the other boy, about one thing. And not even with *both* of them about one thing. But with both of them, about two *different* things. What could either of them have said? "He was crankier with you about your thing than he was with me about mine?"

Hardly.

So they sat quietly on the bus, halfway back, Henri by the open window, Pascal by the aisle.

The bus wasn't full — maybe two-thirds. And all types of people. Men, women, a few kids. Farmers, labourers, even a couple of men who looked like they'd just walked out of the office, who were sitting right in front of the boys.

The driver had the radio playing. Loudly. Loud enough to be heard over the sound of the groaning engine and the jarring road. But it wasn't music. It was talking. Or rather, it sounded more like a sermon. Like a much angrier version of one of Father Michel's sermons. The same coffee-voiced man Pascal had heard a few days before.

"Believe me, it won't be long now," he was saying. "The day of reckoning is just around the corner. So I tell you, my good friends, above all, make sure you're ready. There will only be a limited time to act and to do what needs to be done, because once they scurry back into the shadows, they'll be much, *much* harder to catch. Impossible, perhaps. So make sure you do it right the first time. You know what I'm talking about."

Feeling prickles of worry on the back of his neck, Pascal looked around the bus. Some of the other passengers were nodding in agreement. One man muttered something about filthy cockroaches.

Over on the opposite side of the bus, a woman, perhaps his parents' age or a little older, crossed herself and prayed as she looked out the window. At least, Pascal assumed she was praying. Usually when someone crossed themselves and then said something that couldn't be heard, with their lips barely moving, they were praying.

Her eyes met his as she did a quick scope of the bus. Pascal wasn't really sure what he was expecting her to do — smile or nod, perhaps. But what he didn't expect to see was such a confusing expression. Fear, blank emptiness, a warning to look away. Now. Please. And all at once.

And still the coffee-voiced man on the radio was preaching. The way he was talking, these cockroaches were the most terrifying and evil things anyone had ever met. Dirty, greedy, impossible to get rid of.

"This guy knows what's what," the bus driver said loudly. A short man, balding on top, a thin moustache. Sunglasses that seemed too big for his face. "I just hope the right people are listening to this."

"Excuse me," called out one of the office men in front of the boys. "Excuse me, driver?"

His friend shook his head. "Let it go," he muttered.

"Why should I? It's disgusting! He should turn it off!"

The driver was checking the man out in the mirror. Watching. "It stays on," he called. "My bus, my radio."

"We've paid our fare," the office man called back. "We're your passengers, and we'd like you to turn it down, please."

"Hey!" someone shouted from the back of the bus. "Who put you in charge? If you don't like what's on the radio, you know where the door is!"

The office man half-stood as he turned in his seat. "Listen, this isn't any of your business. I just asked him politely to turn down the —"

"No! Enough!" the man shouted back. Now he was standing too. His eyes bulging. So angry. Angry enough to make the woman across the bus cross herself again and pray some more. "Enough of telling us what to do!"

"Don't worry, he won't be doing that for much longer," said yet another voice. Then, to the office man, this latest person said, "I know where you live, François Otengo. Just think about that before you open your mouth again, you snake."

"I told you to leave it," François's friend muttered. "Now look."

François had crossed his arms and was glaring out the front window of the bus. "Someone had to say something," he answered.

And meanwhile the bus driver had turned up the volume on the radio. It was now so loud that the speakers were distorting. This just made the announcer sound even angrier, even more mad.

"I know we've been talking about this for some time now, but believe me, it's not going to be talk for too much longer. The time for action is coming. Are you ready to do what has to be done for your country? For *your* Rwanda?"

"Can you stop the bus, please?" François said, suddenly standing up. "I'd rather walk."

"It's not safe to stop here," the driver said.

"What do you mean, it's not safe? Stop the bus! Now!"

The angry man at the back was getting involved again. "Let him out," he called. "Let them both out. Snakes don't deserve a bus to ride in."

That was all it took. The driver swerved hard to the side of the road, startling two women who were walking along the verge with huge bundles of sticks on their heads.

"Thank you," François said, and he and his friend climbed down from the bus. Standing beside the open door, he said, "I just want you to know —"

That was all he got to say before the door was closed in their faces. The bus groaned and juddered, then pulled away from the side of the road. Pascal looked back. The two men were standing, watching the bus leave.

The woman across the aisle was crossing herself and praying again.

And the man at the back of the bus was laughing.

So was the driver.

"Did you see the army truck back in Ruhengeri?" Henri suddenly asked. "And the soldiers?"

"I've never seen them around here before," Pascal said. "Why do you think they're here? Is there a war on?"

Henri shrugged. "But it's exciting, don't you think? I kept looking at them and wondering if one of them was my brother."

"I thought Oliver was a plainclothes soldier."

"Yeah, I know, but still . . ."

And it was raining again.

Wednesday 17 March 1999

Wait — so you didn't know? All this time, while you were hearing the radio announcer talking about cockroaches, you didn't realize they were talking about people? Tutsi people?

Us kids never talked about whether someone was Hutu or Tutsi or Twa or whatever. We didn't even think all that much about being Rwandan. We were just kids, doing stuff kids do. You know, like they do everywhere.

It's incredible. Remarkable.

What is?

The way they were talking on the radio. Just . . . hatred. Actually encouraging people to . . . It's beyond belief.

I guess so. But back then, it was just how things were.

But the lady crossing herself on the bus, and the man and his friend — they knew what was coming, didn't they? And your next-door neighbours, too. They all knew what was coming.

No.

No?

No one knew what was coming. Or at least, they didn't expect it to be the way it was, I suppose. If we'd known that, do you think we would have stayed? Do you think my parents would have stayed in Agabande a single day longer if they'd known what was going to happen?

Where would they have gone? If they *had* known, I mean.

That's the thing, isn't it? Where *could* they have gone?

Pascal, it's time to stop for today.

Okay.

Are you happy to stop?

Sure.

You don't want to . . .

To keep talking about it? I never wanted to talk about it in the first place. That was you and Monsieur Baume, remember?

Yes. I remember. Anyway, we do need to finish the week. Monsieur Baume was quite firm about that.

If you say so.

Very well . . . Tomorrow, then? Same time and place?

If you say so.

I do. I'll see you tomorrow, Pascal.

Thursday 18 March 1999

Come in, Pascal. You're a little late.

Sorry.

Okay. How are you today? Are you well?

I guess.

The teachers say that you're having a better week.

So they're talking about me behind my back? That's good to know.

They're concerned about you, that's all.

They don't need to be concerned about me. I'm tough.

I have no doubt about that.

I'll cope.

Sure, but we don't want you to just "cope." We want you to feel well, Pascal. And happy.

I'm well. I just want to get this done. It's just today and tomorrow, right?

I'll be talking to Monsieur Baume, and making my recommendation.

And what will you tell him?

Well, we've got to get through today and tomorrow yet.

"Get through?" . . . Oh, believe me, this is nothing.

All right, then let's get started.

Agabande, Rwanda

A little triangle of steel rod hung on a chain next to the confessional booth in the corner of the empty church. In fact, it wasn't really even a booth. Basically a couple of chairs in the corner of the room with a short section of brush fence propped up between them.

Pascal struck the triangle with the shorter piece of rod that was tied to it, and a high-pitched clang rang through the church. It was so much louder than Pascal had expected it to be.

The door beside the altar opened, but only some of the way, and Pascal saw a dark shape as someone peeked out. Then the door opened the rest of the way and Father Michel emerged, smoothing the wrinkles from the purple sash around his neck.

"Good afternoon, Pascal. Can I help you?"

"I want to do a confession. If that's all right."

"You want to *do* a confession? Do you mean you wish to *make* a confession?"

"If that's the proper way to say it."

"Close enough. Very well." Father Michel gestured towards the chairs. "Take a seat, boy. No, not that one — that's mine. The other one."

"Sorry."

Pascal sat in the chair on the right, and was amazed that such a small piece of fence could block so much of his view. After a moment he heard Father Michel take a deep breath.

"All right, we can begin."

"Um . . ." Pascal said. Uncertain.

A sigh from the priest behind the fence.

"Do you remember how it goes? 'Bless me, Father, for I have sinned.'"

"Sorry," Pascal said. "Bless me, Father, for I have sinned."

"How long has it been since your last confession?"

"It's been a . . . It's been a very long time since my last confession."

"How long is a very long time?"

"Um . . ."

"Have you *ever* made your confession before?"

Pascal shook his head, then remembered that Father Michel couldn't see him. "No, I haven't. Is that a problem?"

"God welcomes all sinners. So if you're ready, let's begin — I'm sure we're going to have a lot to get through. What do you wish to confess?"

Pascal thought for a second. If he tried really hard, he could come up with a very long list of things to own up to. But no, today was about the extra big things — lying to Mama about the M&Ms, but especially stealing the Hershey Kisses. All the other stuff could wait for another time. As it was, the sins he was going to confess would make Father Michel think he was the worst of all the sinners he'd taken confession from all week.

"There's two things," Pascal began.

"That's all? Are you sure? Very well. What's the first one?"

"I told a lie. That's the first sin I want to tell you about — that I told a lie."

"I see. Go on," Father Michel said.

"It wasn't a big lie."

"It doesn't matter. Any lie — *any* lie — is like spitting in the face of God," Father Michel replied. "It doesn't matter how small."

"Oh." This sounded like a problem to Pascal, since he was about to confess that he'd actually told *two* lies.

"But that's why you ask for forgiveness," Father Michel went on. "It allows God to wipe the spit from his own face and forgive you."

"I don't want God to hate me."

"God hates *lies*, but he doesn't hate *liars*. In fact, he loves them. We're all liars, you see."

"Even you, Father?"

"Of course. After all, I am human, just like you. But as long as we confess the sin of lying and ask God for forgiveness, all can be well. So tell me, what was your lie?"

Even after everything Father Michel had just said, it felt silly to say it out loud.

A deep breath. Then the plunge. "I told Mama that the store didn't have any M&Ms. But it did."

"I see . . ." Father Michel said, in a way that made it very clear that he didn't see at all. "Could you maybe tell me a little more about these . . . What were they?"

"M&Ms. They're a chocolate candy from America."

"I see."

"They're all these different colours, but they all taste the same."

"I see," Father Michel said slowly. "So if you could explain what happened, that might be useful . . ."

"We ate them. We bought them, but then we ate them on the way home, and when I got home Mama wondered where they were. So I told her that Mr. Ingabire didn't have any at the store. Which wasn't true. Because he did."

Even from the other side of the screen, Pascal could hear the smile in Father Michel's voice. "I think it's probably all right," he said. "I'm sure God forgives you. Actually, I know he does, so —"

"There was the other lie," Pascal interrupted.

"Oh, of course, there were two. What was the second?"

"I had to go back to the store, and I told Mr. Ingabire that I'd forgotten to bring any money, but I only told him that because I wanted him to go out the back of the shop."

"I'm sorry, but I don't really —"

"And that's when I did the stealing."

"What did you steal?" Father Michel asked.

"A packet of Hershey Kisses."

"A packet of what?"

"Hershey Kisses. It's another kind of candy from America."

"Chocolate again?"

"Yes."

"You know, maybe I'll just tell you to stay away from chocolate," Father Michel said, the smile back in his voice.

"It seems that chocolate plays a part in most of your temptations!"

"I feel really bad," Pascal said. "I only told that lie because I was scared of what Mama would say."

"Well, being scared of your mother is nothing compared to an eternity spent in hell, Pascal."

"Can you go to hell just for telling a lie?" He already knew the answer, but he had to ask.

"Is telling a lie a sin?" Father Michel asked.

What a question! Of course it was. "Yes, Father."

"So there you are. And of course you feel bad — that's your conscience reminding you that you've committed a terrible sin in the eyes of God. So the first thing — do you still have the candy?"

"No," Pascal replied. "We ate it. All of it."

"Who was the other person? Was it your brother?"

"No, it was someone you probably don't know. He doesn't come to church. His name's Henri."

"Oh yes, I know Henri," Father Michel said. "Or rather, I know his father. He's had a terrible time in the last couple of years, with his wife and so on . . . Henri's mother. A fine woman."

"She died."

"Yes, I know. Terrible. So considering you stole after you lied —"

"I feel awful."

"Well, that's because you've done an awful thing."

"Does God hate me now?"

"I already told you, God doesn't hate the sinner — he

hates the *sin*. Do you see the difference?"

"I think so."

"Very well. I'm going to pray with you now, Pascal. Are you ready?"

"Do I have to do anything?"

"No. Just close your eyes and listen." Father Michel's voice changed slightly. More mechanical. "God the Father of mercies, through the death and resurrection of his Son, has forgiven your sins. In the name of the Father, and of the Son and of the Holy Spirit. Say that last part, Pascal."

"Father, Son and Holy Spirit," Pascal repeated.

"Very good. Go in peace." The chair scraped against the concrete floor as Father Michel stood up.

"Is that it?" Pascal asked.

"Yes, that's it. Why? Do you want more? You're forgiven. That's good, isn't it?"

"Yes, I know, but . . . but don't I have to do Hail Mary or something? I think that's what Mama and Papa do."

"I'm surprised your parents remember any of it. I don't recall seeing them in confession for quite a while."

"There's a big church in Ruhengeri," Pascal said. "I saw it today. Maybe Papa does confession there. Do they even do confession at that one?"

"Of course. But why would he go all the way to Ruhengeri, just to go to confession? Especially considering he comes to Mass here every Sunday."

"Because he works in Ruhengeri," Pascal answered.

"Of course, I remember now. He's been there for a couple of months, yes? At the government office?"

"Yes, right across the road from the church. He looks after the trucks and vans and things. He's very important," Pascal said, wondering if pride was okay when it was your father you were proud of and not yourself.

"Oh, I'm sure he is," Father Michel said. The chair scraped again as he stood, and the sound echoed around the empty church. "Go in peace, child. But don't forget to make amends. That's important."

"Make amends? What's that?"

"Oh, yes. You should tell Mr. Ingabire what you've done, and find a way to pay him back. And of course you must continue to show remorse."

"What does that mean?"

"Remorse? You have to actually *be* sorry, and determine not to do it again. And you must come back here. You must continue to confess. Confessing just the once isn't enough."

"Thank you, Father Michel."

"Of course. I'll see you again soon."

Going through the front door of the church, Pascal stepped aside to let a man enter. Even without the machete, Pascal recognized Smiley-man from outside Mr. Ingabire's shop the day before. But if Smiley-man recognized Pascal, he didn't show it. He just walked in like he might need to confess something, but if he couldn't, it wouldn't matter.

Then, as Pascal passed by the little bell shelter near the gate, he found himself wondering what Smiley-man was confessing to Father Michel. Would he know the words? And since he was a grown-up and not a kid, would he have to do Hail Marys for whatever he'd done?

141

And would he show remorse?

There was no way to know.

"Pascal!" Father Oscar was calling, waving to him from the concrete step in front of Father Michel's office. A hoe in his good hand, a newly dug garden beside him.

Pascal wandered across. Feeling light, after confessing his terrible sins.

"So, you came to see me again?" Father Oscar said, smiling. "Twice in one week!"

"No, I came and did confession with Father Michel."

"Ah." A knowing nod. "It's good to confess our sins."

"Do you do confession?"

"Of course."

"Is it because you're scared of going to hell?"

Father Oscar twisted his mouth sideways as he thought. "No."

"You're not scared of hell?"

"I think hell would be awful. Worse than awful. The very worst. But I'm not scared of it."

Strange. "Why not?"

"Because I'm not going to go there. Because of that," he said, pointing at the crucifix above the office door. "Jesus, you see . . ." He needed to say nothing more.

"What's hell like, anyway?" Pascal asked.

"It's . . . I don't know. I've never been there, of course. I mean, it's . . . hell. It's not nice."

"I know, but is it really a dark place underground with a fire that never goes out? That's what Sister Odette told us in Sunday School."

Father Oscar twisted his mouth sideways again. Finally: "No."

"It's not?"

"I don't think so, no."

Pascal sighed. "That's good. Because that would be horrible."

"Wait — I'm not saying that hell isn't horrible. Hell *is* horrible. But I think hell is something much worse than underground fires for all of eternity."

"What is it, then? What's it look like?"

"Oh, Pascal, I have no idea what it *looks* like. But I think I know what it is. It's a place without God. It's a life without God. It's a place where God can't show his face. It's a place where we have decided that evil is a better way than good."

"I don't . . . "

"Pascal, do you listen to the radio?"

Pascal shook his head. "I'm not allowed."

"I worry. I listen to the radio and I worry."

"About what?"

"The future. About hell. I feel that hell will be with us before too long."

"But only bad people go to hell, and they go there after they die, don't they? If they've never done confession or prayed to Jesus and Mary."

"That's true, but I do worry that many good people will know hell before they die, Pascal."

"Excuse me, Father Oscar." Another of the priests, Brother Gilles, had walked up behind them. "Father Michel wants to speak with you. Up at the church."

Pascal turned. In the door of the church stood Father Michel, watching. As soon as he saw that his message had been passed on to Father Oscar, he turned and went back into the church.

Father Oscar leaned the hoe against the wall and looked at his hands. Both of them, but mainly his left one. The one that wasn't a claw. "Not too dirty," he muttered as he brushed them on his backside. "I don't know how long I'll be, Pascal," he said.

"I'll wait."

"No, I think you should go now."

Father Oscar hurried off up the slight hill to the church, with Brother Gilles close behind. Trailing behind him like a goatherd.

Pascal looked down at the piles of weeds lying along in front of the garden beds. They'd need picking up. It was something he could do. Something to help. Something to help Jesus.

It took him maybe ten minutes to scrape all the weeds together into one larger pile.

It took about the same number of minutes for Father Oscar to emerge from his meeting with Father Michel. He crossed the yard to where Pascal was putting the last few stray weeds on the pile.

"Pascal. I told you to go." Father Oscar's voice was tense. Serious.

"I wanted to help."

"Yes, but I told you to go."

"But, Father Oscar, I picked up all the —"

"I know you did, and thank you. But I'm serious about this — you need to go home, *now*. Besides, it's starting to rain again."

"All right." Feeling a little hurt. Unappreciated. "I guess I'll see you tomorrow. Or maybe the next day."

"I think that maybe . . . Yes, Pascal. In a few days. It will be good to see you then. But right now . . . Goodbye, my young friend." Father Oscar placed his good hand on Pascal's shoulder, squeezed it gently. "And may God go with you."

Pascal reached the bottom of the hill, walked beneath the wide cover of the strangler fig. Under there the raindrops were fewer, but heavier. They gathered together on the broad, waxy leaves, then fell as much larger, heavier drops.

Mr. Ingabire's front door was open, which meant his shop was open. Which meant that Mr. Ingabire was in there. Which meant this was Pascal's chance to make things right. To go in there and tell what he'd done. To apologize. To promise to repay him. To say he'd never do anything like that again. To ask for forgiveness.

But at the same time, it was too easy to find reasons not to. He had no money to give Mr. Ingabire. He couldn't return what he'd stolen. He should probably tell his parents first. All good reasons. All excellent excuses. No, better to go home. Think about it, deal with it another time. Maybe on a day when it wasn't raining. If he went in there now, he'd only take mud onto that nice clean floor, and that would just make Mr. Ingabire cross. Besides, it was probably almost time for his afternoon chores. He should get home.

With the rain still falling steadily, Pascal jogged across the road, dodging a couple of cars and motorbikes and a number of puddles along the way. Then it was through the gap between Mr. Ingabire's store and the clinic, heading for the shortcut up through the forest to his house. As he ran through the gap, he almost collided with Miss Uwazuba. She was walking down from the market, the two string bags hanging from each hand bulging with fruit and vegetables.

"Pascal."

"Hello, Miss. You weren't at school today."

"No. No, I wasn't. I'm sorry. I was . . ."

"Were you sick?"

"In a way."

He noticed her knuckles, pale from the effort of holding the heavy shopping bags. Rain streaked her face, dotted her hair. At least it *looked* like rain streaking her cheeks.

"Miss, is everything all right?" Remembering too late how he'd got in trouble the last time he asked her that.

"Yes, Pascal. Well, yes, in a sense, I suppose. What I mean is . . ." She stopped. Was her chin crumpling up? Was she starting to cry?

The bags must have been too heavy for her.

"Would you like me to carry some of your shopping?" Pascal offered.

Now Miss Uwazuba looked like she was going to cry properly. "I'll be fine, Pascal. But thank you, I'll be . . . Actually, I would absolutely love it if you would carry a couple of my shopping bags for me," she said suddenly. "I don't live very far up that way. Only five minutes or so."

Pascal swallowed hard as he took two of the bags from her. It had just struck him that he was about to see where his teacher lived. And it was in the same direction as his house. All this time, he'd never known how close they lived to each other.

"So, do you live near here, Pascal?" Miss Uwazuba asked.

"Kind of," he answered. "Up there." He pointed with his chin, since his hands were busy with the two very heavy bags of shopping. The string handles were cutting into his fingers. But he wasn't going to stop, or even ask for a break. He'd have carried those bags all the way to Miss Uwazuba's house even if she'd lived in Ruhengeri. Even Kigali.

"Thanks for helping," she said. "Are you all right?"

"I'm fine." Apart from the tips of my fingers going numb, he thought. And the rainwater running down into my eyes. The rain was lighter now, but still drizzling enough to be annoying.

"Well, I appreciate you offering," Miss Uwazuba said. "After the week I've had, I really needed someone to show me some kindness, so . . . " There was a tiny catch in her voice, right at the end of the sentence. "Sorry."

Pascal wasn't quite sure what she was apologizing for.

"This is my house here," she said as they approached a small, tidy mud brick place, maybe only one or two rooms. A neat little garden out the front. A path to the front door, lined with more of the mud bricks. And a view across towards the mountains, where the gorillas lived and the tourists visited.

The sound of an engine drifted to them from beyond

the next bend in the road. It was accompanied by the sound of voices. Men's voices. Were they singing, chanting or just yelling? Maybe all three at once.

Then the truck appeared. A small pickup with three men in the cab, and six or seven in the back, some with long poles, some with farm tools. As the truck jolted and bucked and spluttered past Miss Uwazuba's house, some of the men called out. But what were they saying? It was hard to know, exactly, they shouted it with such force. Something about cleaning? Something about cockroaches? Very weird, all this bug talk at the moment.

"Pigs," Miss Uwazuba muttered as the truck disappeared over the low crest in the road. "Come on."

She walked up the path to the door, stopped, turned, gestured for Pascal to follow. He was still at the beginning of the path, uncertain how far he should go. This was his teacher's house. Miss Uwazuba. The beautiful lady named after the sun.

"Pascal! Come on."

He went up the path after her. She faced the door, sighed heavily and opened it. "Come in, Pascal. Just put the bags over there."

"On the table?"

"Yes. Thank you so much."

He crossed the main room to the corner that served as the kitchen, judging by the red plastic washing-up bowl on the trestle table. He lifted the bags onto the table, wriggled his fingers, trying to get some feeling into them.

A clean place. Not rich, but proud. One door into

148

another room — probably the bedroom — and a back door. A chair, a wooden bench, a side table, some pictures on the wall, a crucifix above the front door. One of the pictures was a framed photograph. Miss Uwazuba and a man. They looked happy. Broad, shining smiles.

"Pascal?"

"Sorry, Miss, I didn't hear what you said."

"I said, would you like some water? Or . . . No, wait! How about this?" She put her own bags down, then opened a wooden chest beside the table. From it, she took a bottle of Fanta. Held it out.

"For me?"

Smiling. "Yes, of course. To thank you."

Taking it reverently. "But it's Fanta."

"I know it's Fanta. Delicious, huh?"

"U-huh."

"I don't drink the stuff anyway. I kept it for my . . ." Suddenly her eyes were welling up again. "Just take it, Pascal. Please. It won't be very cold, but it's still Fanta. Here." She dug around in a box of cutlery for a moment, finally pulling out a bottle opener. A twist of her wrist, and the cap flew off, landing on the other side of the room. She giggled. "Here. Enjoy."

The tingle down his throat, the sharpness of the bubbles on the back of his lips. And it was all his. No need to share it with anyone.

"Good?" Miss Uwazuba asked.

"U-huh." He nodded. Then he hiccupped, which made Miss Uwazuba laugh again. It was nice.

"Sorry," he said.

"For what? It has the same effect on my fiancé . . . Well . . ." Followed by that look again. The welling-up look. "Just don't let it spoil your dinner."

Dinner! What time was it?

"Can I take the rest of this with me?" he asked, holding up the Fanta.

"Of course. Why wouldn't you —"

"Bye, Miss. I have to go."

The closer Pascal got to home, the slower he walked. He knew he had to hurry, but at the same time, some invisible force was dragging him back. It was the knowledge that Papa would probably be home by now, and he wasn't going to be happy. He'd definitely have something to say about Pascal catching a ride to Ruhengeri with a truck full of armed men. And something else to say about Henri and his rudeness. And possibly a few words about him being home so late.

Papa was at the side of the house as Pascal arrived home. He was repairing the little fence that was supposed to keep Iggy out of the front garden. He had a row of nails clamped between his lips, which made it difficult for him to call Pascal across. But he somehow managed it with a kind of grunt.

Pascal wasn't in any doubt.

"Yes, Papa?"

Papa carefully took the nails from his mouth.

"Do you have any change for me?"

"Yes, Papa. It's in my pocket."

"Give it to your mother when you go inside. Do you have anything else to give me? An apology, for instance?"

"I'm sorry, Papa. I just wanted to surprise you, and see where you work."

"You did surprise me. You also surprised your mother."

"How?"

"Did you tell her you were planning to go to another town today?"

Pascal shook his head.

"So imagine her surprise when I told her that you turned up at the place where I work."

"Oh." He hadn't thought of that. But *now* he was thinking about it, and it wasn't a pleasant thought. "Is she cross?"

Papa didn't answer. He simply put the nails back between his lips and chuckled.

Oh dear, Pascal thought. That wasn't a good chuckle.

It turned out that Papa was right. Mama wasn't happy.

"Sit down there," she said, pointing at one of the kitchen chairs.

"But —"

"Sit!"

He sat.

"Ruhengeri? Really? On your own?"

He shook his head. "I wasn't alone, Mama. Henri came with me."

"Don't get smart. If school's not on for some reason, you come straight home. Yes? I shouldn't have to tell you that."

"Yes, Mama."

"You idiot," Jean-Baptiste said as he came through the kitchen. He cuffed Pascal on the back of the head. Laughed. "Ruhengeri!" He laughed again.

"That's enough, Jean-Baptiste," Mama said. "Now go and do your chores, both of you. It's getting dark. Then you can come in and set the table, Pascal."

"But setting the table isn't one of my . . . Yes, Mama," he said when she gave him one of her special warning stares. The kind that didn't make an appearance all that often.

When he'd finished his evening outside chores — making sure to give Papa a wide berth — and had gone back inside to set the table, Pascal took one of the empty Primus bottles from beside the back door, rinsed it out with water from the tank and refilled it. Then, after checking that no one was watching, he climbed through the little round hole into his water tank hideout. Would anyone notice if he didn't come inside, he wondered as he drank some of the water. It tasted slightly of beer. He didn't mind. That made it a little like drinking real beer. And it still tasted better than the sugary honey-lemon "whisky" he and Henri kept in there.

Perhaps that was it for his punishment. A telling-off, some extra chores and the knowledge that his parents were pretty disappointed in him.

"Pascal?" Mama was calling from the back door. "Where are you? It's time for dinner."

He didn't answer. He couldn't give away the position of the hideout. It didn't really matter — most times she'd go and look somewhere else, and that's when he'd come out of hiding. It was important. No one could ever know the position of his and Henri's hideout.

"That boy . . ." he heard Mama say to herself. Then the door closed, and he counted to ten before emerging into the falling darkness.

It was late, maybe nine o'clock, and Pascal was feeling frustrated. He was frustrated because his little sister hadn't been sent to bed yet. It was as if she thought that now she was five she could stay up as late as she liked. And Mama was doing nothing to make her think otherwise. And since Pascal was still smarting after being told off by his parents, he didn't want to be the one to ask if it was time for Nadine to go to bed.

She was lying on the floor playing with Macaron, while Pascal tried to scratch some kind of tread into the wheel of his tractor using a blunt knife he'd taken from the kitchen. If only he had something sharp to use. A proper pocket knife like Henri's, perhaps.

Meanwhile Jean-Baptiste was lying on the floor with his feet on one of the chairs. His usual spot. What a strange brother. He was humming to himself. And above his face, at arm's length, he was tearing a piece of paper into small pieces. Each piece he tore, he'd allow to fall towards his face, drifting like a dead leaf. Then, as it got close, he would puff air from his cheeks, and try to blow the paper fragment off course. *Hum, hum, rip, hum, puff, hum, hum, rip, hum, puff . . .*

Mama was stitching a button on to Nadine's Sunday dress, and Papa sat in his usual reading spot in the corner, gently tapping the side of his head with the pointer finger of his right hand.

Nadine didn't seem to be getting even slightly tired, and Pascal was about to give up and go to bed anyway when the knock on the door came. Mama glanced up at the door, then at Papa, then at each of the children, then back at the door.

The knock came again, a little louder this time, more determined. Mama looked at Papa again and raised her eyebrows, just a little. Just a flicker. The tip of Papa's finger remained beside his right ear, but now it was completely still. They were like a painting of a family, frozen on a canvas.

It wasn't unusual for people to drop in, even late at night. Some, like Mrs. Malolo, wouldn't even knock. She'd just walk in announcing "It's only me!" at any old time, day or night. Mrs. N'Dranda would tap twice, then open the door and poke her head into the front room. Or more often the back door, into the kitchen. So it wasn't the knock that Pascal found strange. It was the fact that his parents just looked at one another. Neither of them moved. Neither of them seemed likely to stand up and open the door as they would ordinarily have done. It was as if they'd forgotten how to move, how to speak.

Nadine was the first to break the silence. "Can me and Macaron answer the door?" she asked, leaping up.

The moment she said this, it was as if life had been breathed into their frozen painting. Papa replied first, mainly because Mama was too busy sucking in air between her teeth. "No, it's late. Boys, take your sister and put her

154

to bed," he said. "And you go to bed as well. Both of you."

"But I hate going to bed at the same time as —" Jean-Baptiste began to say, but when Mama growled at him, he must have decided that this was no time to be talking back, and his mouth snapped shut.

"Come on, Nadine," Pascal muttered. "Grab your stupid doll."

Nadine knew something important was happening. She must have known — why else would she have ignored the comment about Macaron and willingly followed Pascal? She didn't complain. And that wasn't like her at all.

As soon as they were in their bedroom, Pascal pointed at Nadine's bed. "Get in," he ordered as he and Jean-Baptiste took up a good listening position near the door.

"But you have to tuck me in!" Nadine whined. "That's how it works — *I* tuck Macaron in first, then you tuck *me* in."

"Shut up!" Jean-Baptiste hissed.

"I'll do all that once you're in bed," Pascal told Nadine. "Now shush!"

"Why do I have to shush? You're not the boss of me!"

"Shut up!" Jean-Baptiste snapped again, and this time Nadine got the message. She pouted and started muttering quietly to Macaron about her horrible brothers.

By now, Papa had opened the front door, and was speaking with the person who'd knocked. Pascal recognized Dr. Singh's voice immediately. Thanks to Nadine's complaining, Pascal had missed the very beginning of the conversation.

"It's madness down there in Kigali," Dr. Singh was

saying. "I spoke with a friend from the women's hospital, and he said that no one knows what to do."

"When did it happen?" Mama asked.

"About an hour ago, maybe more."

Papa's voice was low, and deadly serious. "Are they sure he's dead?"

"I think so. The radio said that there was a fireball in the air, then the plane crashed into the palace. There was a big explosion when it hit the ground so yes, I'd say he's definitely dead."

"Please, Ravindra, sit down," Papa said. "Have they said who's to blame?"

"It's too early to know," Dr. Singh answered, "but if I had to guess, I'd say it was the Hutus."

"No!" Mama exclaimed. "No, that can't be right! He was Hutu himself! They wouldn't kill one of their own!"

"Of course they would," Papa said, his voice flat. Stony. "They would if they could pin the blame on someone else."

"So what happens now?" asked Mama. Pascal couldn't see her, since he was still standing in the dark of their bedroom, tucked away in the shadow of the door, but he could sense her fear just as clearly as if he'd been standing beside her and looking up into her face.

"What happens now?" Papa replied. "We wait."

"Wait and watch," Dr. Singh added. "Especially the watching."

"I wonder what RTLM are saying," Papa said.

"Don't!" Mama said. "Please, Moises, we don't want to hear what they have to say."

156

"We must."

Pascal heard a click and a hiss and a few seconds of garbled voices cutting in and out as Papa switched on the little transistor radio and tuned into the right station.

"Of course, we've been waiting patiently for this day for some time," said the scratchy voice of the man on the radio. "But now, at last, the waiting is over. Don't waste any time, because there's none to waste. We all know about cockroaches, and how hard they are to get rid of. I've said this over and over, haven't I? You kill one, but then there's always another five or ten or a hundred hidden in the shadows. You step on one, you crush it, and you think the job is done, but then you move a box or a chest or a tin of cookies, and there you find more, hiding and waiting to slink around after you turn out the light. Big ones, little ones, parents, children. And be under no illusion, my fellow Rwandans, little cockroaches grow up to be —"

"What are you doing?" Pascal heard Papa say as the radio went silent. "Why did you turn it off? I was listening to that!"

"Why? Why would you want to listen to that poison? No, I've heard enough."

Mama's voice was brittle. Sad? Frightened? Angry? Pascal couldn't be sure which. "I refuse to listen to any more of this hatefulness."

"I know it's not nice to listen to, but we have to know what's happening," Papa insisted. "We have to know what to do next."

"You have to stay alert," Dr. Singh said. "That's all you can do, I think."

"Well, I won't be intimidated," Papa said. "None of us will. Besides, look at this."

"Your ID card? What good is that?" Dr. Singh asked.

"Read that, there. Hutu."

"And you?" Dr. Singh asked.

"No," Mama replied. "Tutsi."

"Listen to me," Dr. Singh said. But then his voice became too quiet for Pascal to hear.

"Do you think it's bad?" Jean-Baptiste asked Pascal.

"I don't know. It sounds bad. Doesn't it?"

"I guess. I mean, Dr. Singh came all the way up here," Jean-Baptiste said as they heard the door close and the clinic van start up in front of their house.

Nadine hadn't said anything for a while. When he checked, Pascal expected to see her fast asleep with her eyes closed.

But her eyes were wide open. "Pascal," she whispered. "I'm scared."

"Don't be stupid," Jean-Baptiste said. "There's nothing to be frightened of."

But Pascal wasn't so sure. There was something about the way she'd said it that chilled him.

"Jean-Baptiste's right," he said. "There's nothing to be scared about."

But he didn't even believe that himself.

A little later, Mama came in to tuck them all in. By then, Nadine had gone to sleep, but the boys were still awake.

"Mama, what's going on?" Jean-Baptiste asked when she eased the bedroom door open.

"Don't worry about it," she whispered. "It's nothing."

It didn't sound like nothing, Pascal thought. It sounded like a whole lot more than nothing.

"What was the man on the radio saying?" Jean-Baptiste asked.

"I told you, it was nothing."

"And Dr. Singh? Why was he here?"

"Not so loud — you'll wake your sister. Dr. Singh had to talk to Papa about something."

Pascal considered this. Something couldn't be nothing. And if there was nothing, then it couldn't be something.

Mama was working her way around the room, checking each of the mosquito nets. "Anyway," she said, her voice suddenly brighter, "how would you like another day off school tomorrow?"

Strangely, that didn't sound as appealing as it might have.

Agabande, Rwanda

Thursday 7 April 1994

No school. But for Pascal, that didn't mean a day of climbing trees and working on his tractor. It meant chores, chores and more chores. And it meant doing those chores with Jean-Baptiste. That was never much fun. But when it was all day, it was like torture. Not because of the work — because of Jean-Baptiste. Whining, complaining, pranking. Pascal was sure he was just trying to irritate Papa until he told him to get lost.

There was a large section of garden that Papa wanted cleared so he could put in a few more plantain trees. He wasn't at work either. Having him work beside the boys made it almost bearable. At least, it did while he was there. For some reason he left them every half an hour or so to go inside. Then, after a while, what he was doing became clear, when he brought the radio outside and put it on the corner of the tank stand. Turned it way down. Would go over to it every now and then, pick it up, hold it close to his ear. Listen with a frown. Make some disapproving sound as he turned it off.

"What are you listening to?" Jean-Baptiste asked. "Can we have some music, at least?"

"No," Papa said. "Keep chopping. Actually, can you take

these branches and weeds over to the goat? She'd like them."

She did like them. It was impossible to know this from looking at her eyes, because they were blank and expressionless, but the speed with which she demolished the garden scraps told a different story.

"Papa, why aren't you at work today?" Pascal enquired. He hoped that he and Henri hadn't got Papa into trouble with his boss by going to Ruhengeri. Maybe he'd been sacked.

"No work today," Papa replied. "There, do that patch next, Jean-Baptiste. Don't be slack. Honestly . . ."

Lunch was a short affair. No one said very much. Mama brought the food out, then Papa and the boys sat on the grass to eat. Pascal and Jean-Baptiste didn't say anything, because it was clear that Papa was deep in thought. He got up three times during lunch to listen to the radio. But he wouldn't let the boys listen.

"Nothing for you to worry about," he told them.

But he wasn't a very good liar.

Besides, no one had asked him if they should be worried.

"All right, that's enough for today," Papa said around the middle of the afternoon. "Thanks, boys, you've worked hard." Jean-Baptiste didn't need to be asked twice. He heard Papa say, "that's enough for today" and he was gone.

"Stay close by!" Papa called after him. Then he pulled up the bottom edge of his T-shirt and wiped his brow with it. The muscles of his stomach gleamed. One day, Pascal thought. One day.

Papa glanced at the sky. "Just beat the rain," he said. "Perfect timing. What are you going to do now?"

Pascal shrugged.

"Whatever it is, stay close, okay?"

"Can I go and play at Henri's house?"

"What did I just say?" Papa replied. "Stay close by."

"Why?"

"Because I said so!"

It wasn't the best answer, but it seemed to be the only one he was going to get. Papa gathered up the machetes and axe and headed back to the house. "Pascal, can you take the radio inside before it rains," he called over his shoulder as he went around the end of the house to where he stored the tools.

The radio was switched off. It took all of Pascal's willpower not to flick it on.

But he didn't.

Later, he'd wish he had.

Pascal sat on the back step, still working on the wheels of his tractor. Tried not to think about Henri's knife, slicing through wood like green banana. Maybe that's what he'd say when his parents asked him what he wanted for his birthday.

"Out of the way, Short-stuff." Jean-Baptiste gave Pascal a clip across the back of the head. It was probably a bit harder than it needed to be. Then, without even waiting for Pascal to move, Jean-Baptiste stepped over him.

"Where are you going?" Pascal asked.

"How is that any of your business?"

Pascal shrugged. "It's not, I guess. But Papa said that we couldn't go anywhere."

"No, he didn't."

"He did! Right after we finished working in the garden!"

"I didn't hear him. Anyway, why would he even say that? As long as we're home in time for dinner, they don't care."

"Well, that's what he said," Pascal argued. "He said, 'Stay around the house.' Or maybe it was, 'Don't leave the house.'"

"Which was it?" Jean-Baptiste asked. "See? You don't even remember. So that means he didn't say it. See ya!"

"Wait! You should ask Mama. Do you want me to ask her for you?"

"Too slow!" Jean-Baptiste called as he dashed off towards the gap in the fence that led to the shortcut to town.

Mama stood in the bedroom doorway. "Dinner will be ready soon," she told Pascal. "I need you and Jean-Baptiste to do your chores."

"I can do mine," Pascal replied. "But do I have to do his?"

Mama appeared puzzled. "Why would you have to do your brother's chores? Has he been making bets with you again?"

Pascal shook his head. "Because I think he's at Kami's house."

How to describe Mama's expression? Horror? Anger? Some other strange combination that had no name?

"Kami's house? Did he ask your father? Because he didn't ask me."

How easy it would be to say "No, he didn't ask anyone."

163

But he couldn't say "I don't know," either, because that would be a lie. And it was only twenty-four hours since he'd confessed to lying and promised God, Jesus, Mary and Father Michel never to do it again.

"Didn't he ask you?" he said at last.

Mama shook her head. Barely containing the rage. Or horror. That terrible, nameless thing.

"He needs to come back now," she said, as much to herself as to Pascal. "Someone needs to get him."

"I'll go."

"No. Your father will have to . . . No, that's no good. He's had to go down to town. It'll be dark soon."

"But I can run," Pascal said. "I'm a good runner, Mama. Strong. I'll go over there, tell him to come home, and be back real quick."

Mama took a deep breath. Closed her eyes and muttered something to herself.

"All right," she said at last. "Can you run all the way there *and* all the way back?"

"Sure," he said. Was that another lie? Probably not. "I'll try, anyway."

"Okay. Straight there, straight back, do you hear me? No Henri, no shop, no climbing trees. I mean it! And . . ." She stopped.

"What is it, Mama?"

"I never thought I'd have to say this, but no talking to anyone you don't know, all right?"

"Yes, Mama."

"All right. Go. Run. And straight back, *with your brother.*"

164

Oh boy, he's going to be in such trouble, Pascal thought, perhaps a little too gleefully.

Down through the shortcut. Raindrops heavy in the undergrowth and the dark, cool places. Lighter up high in the canopy of leaves. Cutting up through the market lane, past the back of the clinic. It was here that Pascal saw Dr. Singh loading boxes into the back of his van. On these boxes were words, names, logos. A pile of boxes stacked beside the van's open back door, and Dr. Singh was sliding them in, pushing them, making them fit.

Pascal stopped. "Dr. Singh?"

Mrs. Singh had just come out of the clinic carrying two bags, and she frowned at Pascal as she handed the bags to her husband. Then she said something to him in a language that Pascal didn't recognize — Indian, perhaps, or maybe English — before throwing another unhappy glance at Pascal and hurrying back inside.

Dr. Singh sighed. "Pascal. What's wrong?"

"Are you going somewhere?"

"Yes."

"Where are you going?"

"Pascal . . . "

"Are you leaving?"

Another sigh. "Yes, Pascal. My wife and I are leaving."

"Leaving? Why?"

"Because it's time to go. Our family are in South Africa. That's where we'll go."

"But why now?"

"It's the right time. It's . . . just the right time."

Pascal didn't know what to say to this. What was it that made this the "right time" for Dr. and Mrs. Singh to leave?

"So who's going to work in the clinic now?"

Dr. Singh's mouth opened and closed a couple of times.

"Is there a new doctor coming?" Pascal asked.

"Pascal, it's not that simple . . . "

It didn't seem like a difficult, not-simple question. But just as it seemed that Dr. Singh was about to reply, he was cut off by his wife, who snapped at him from the back door of the clinic. Again, it was said in a language Pascal didn't know.

"I have to go, Pascal," Dr. Singh said. "I have . . . I still have a lot to do."

Mrs. Singh held the door open for him as he hurried inside. Then she let the door close, and Pascal heard the latch click as she locked it from the inside.

And then, driving far too fast down the lane, came the truck. Bristling with men. Young men. Chanting. A different truck from the one he'd seen outside Miss Uwazuba's house. Most of the men were wearing regular clothes, but a couple of them were wearing what looked like army clothes. Soldiers, with rifles.

Pascal wondered if one of the men in regular clothes was Henri's brother, the plainclothes soldier.

"Pascal?" Mr. Ingabire was at the back of his shop, sweeping. Always sweeping. He looked over the top of his glasses. Frowned.

Pascal, frozen in place. The man he'd stolen from, lied to. Twice.

Mr. Ingabire glanced up and down the lane. "What are you doing here?"

"I'm going to get my brother," Pascal replied. "I have to take him home."

"I should think so, too," Mr. Ingabire said. "Listen, Pascal, you shouldn't be out. It's dangerous."

"Why?"

"Your parents haven't told you?"

Pascal shook his head.

"Nothing?"

He shook his head again.

"Pascal, listen to me. Get your brother, and go straight home. And ask your parents to tell you what's going on in Kigali."

Kigali. Where Henri's brother had been living. Maybe he had been one of the men in the truck!

"Are you hearing what I'm saying?" Mr. Ingabire asked. "Pascal? Straight home. I'm serious!"

"Yes, sir."

Mr. Ingabire took one more glance up and down the lane. Then, without another word, he went into his shop and closed the door firmly behind himself.

Pascal knocked on the door of Kami's house and waited. It was getting dark now. Dark and quite cool, almost cold, especially with his shirt damp from the drizzling rain.

Drifting to him from farther back towards town, he heard someone shout something.

A dog barked close by. And from somewhere between

the shouter and the dog was the roar of an engine.

And farther into the distance than all of that, as if it were coming from the mountains all around, was a popping sound. Not regular like a dripping tap. Uneven, in short, irregular bursts.

Now he knocked.

He knocked again.

And then the door flew open.

Kami's older brother Jules stood there, lamplight glistening off his bare shoulders. Tall, muscular. Towering. Intimidating. Behind him, four equally intimidating young men were gathered, squatting on their heels with their backs against the walls. One was sharpening a long machete, the whetstone making a long, screeching *shiiing* with each stroke. Between each one, Pascal could hear the radio. The man with the coffee-coloured voice. But now with a little more crazy to it.

"Yes?" Jules asked, stepping slightly to one side, blocking Pascal's view into the house.

"Is Jean-Baptiste here?"

A tiny shrug. "Who's that?"

"My brother. He's Kami's friend."

"Huh. Yes, I think he's here. Why?"

"I need to talk to him."

"Do you?" Suddenly: "Kami! Your friend's little brother is here."

Kami's brother turned, walked away, returning to the others, leaving Pascal standing all alone and obvious in the open doorway.

168

"How about the lodge?" Pascal heard one of the young men say as Kami's brother sat back down. "That wouldn't be a bad place to —"

"Wait." Kami's brother interrupted him. "Just . . . just wait." He took a long swig from his bottle of Primus. Raised one hand when the other man tried to argue.

Now Jean-Baptiste was crossing the room, his head bowed. Humiliated. He stood close to Pascal, muttered, "What do you want?"

"Mama said you have to come home."

Inside, someone choked on their beer.

"Not so loud!" Jean-Baptiste said. "Why do I have to come home?"

"Because your mommy said so, little man," one of the young guys called out. And any dignity Jean-Baptiste had left seemed to leave his body.

Pascal shrugged. "I don't know. You just do. Dinner, I guess."

Now Kami had joined them. He could barely conceal his disdain for Pascal. "What does *he* want?" he asked Jean-Baptiste.

"Nothing. He was just leaving."

"Jean-Baptiste has to come home. Mama said."

"Shut up!" Jean-Baptiste hissed. Inside the room, there was more laughter. "Tell them I'm eating here. I'll come home later."

"Mama said —"

Kami's brother stood, slowly crossed the room. Placed one hand on Kami's shoulder and pulled him out of the way.

169

"Your brother doesn't want to come home. So why don't you go home and tell your mommy and daddy that? Goodbye."

He closed the door. And as the latch clicked into place, Pascal heard more laughter from inside the house.

But he couldn't hear Jean-Baptiste laughing.

In that space amongst the one thousand hills, the shouting had stopped. The sound of the engine had stopped. The popping in the far distance had stopped.

But the dog was still barking. On and on and on, echoed by other dogs around the valley.

It was much darker now. Too dark to go through the shortcut, even though he knew every step. He'd walked that path in the darkness many times. But none of those other nights had felt like this.

So he stuck to the road, even though it was a little farther. He didn't mind all that much, since that road took him past Miss Uwazuba's house. He hadn't known that until yesterday.

The door to Miss Uwazuba's house was slightly open. This didn't surprise him too much — people in Agabande often left their houses unlocked. In fact, most didn't have locks on their doors at all. But if Miss Uwazuba's front door was open, shouldn't there be some light coming from inside the house? Through the door, through the cracks between the curtains?

He'd seen inside that house just the day before, and he knew that there were only two rooms. Any light in there would have shown up against the dark walls.

No, it wasn't all right to go up the neatly lined path to check if everything was okay. After all, he was just a boy. What could he do anyway? Yesterday she'd seemed very upset about something, and now he could imagine her sitting in the dark, deep in thought. Crying, perhaps. It wasn't his problem. She was a grown-up, and he was a kid. There was nothing he could do to make her feel better.

The N'Drandas' house was a few doors down from Pascal's. And it was their dog, Hubert, who was doing most of the barking. On and on and on. He was over by the far fence, barking at something out of sight farther up the hill. A few doors up, perhaps.

"Hubert!" Pascal called in a loud whisper. "Hubert, what's wrong?"

The dog turned, saw him and bounded across the yard, snarling. Teeth bared. He leapt at the fence, bending it back with his weight. Barking, snarling.

"Hubert! It's me! Calm down!"

Still bounding. Still snarling.

"Hubert!"

The door of the house creaked, cracked open. No lights in the windows of this house either. Just empty, dark spaces. But someone was behind the crack in the door.

"Who is it?" Mr. N'Dranda's voice was low. Little more than a growl. "Who's out there? Don't even think about coming near this house. I'll fight back. I used to be in the army, you know."

"Mr. N'Dranda? It's Pascal."

"Pascal? From up the road?" The door opened slightly

wider. Now a dark shadow was visible through the gap. "What are you doing out there? You shouldn't be outside. It's not safe."

"I'm going home."

"I suggest you hurry. Hubert! Come here and be quiet, dog!"

Another voice joined the conversation. "What are you doing? Who are you talking to?" Mrs. N'Dranda asked her husband.

"Just the boy from up the road. Pascal."

"Pascal?" The door opened even wider again. "You shouldn't be outside. Not tonight. You should go straight back home. And tell your parents to turn on the radio."

"They have been listening to the radio," Pascal told her.

"They have? And they still let you outside?"

"I had to get my brother."

"Where is he?"

"He wouldn't come home," Pascal replied.

"Well, *you* should hurry home, at least," Mrs. N'Dranda said.

"I will," Pascal answered.

The door closed. Pascal heard a rattle as the latch was slid across, and a thump as something was pushed hard against the door.

Meanwhile, Hubert had returned to the far side of the yard and had gone back to barking furiously, desperately, at something up the hill.

Up the hill.

Where Pascal lived.

Pascal pushed their door open all the way. Like Miss Uwazuba's front door, it had been left slightly ajar. No lights. The house was a hollow shell.

Pascal wanted to call out. He wanted to scream. He wanted to bite his lip and stay silent. He wanted to make his presence known, even while he remained silent.

But you can't do all those things at once. He wasn't sure if he could do any of them.

A hiccup. That was all it was in the end. A kind of choking cough, a spasm of his chest, along with a gurgling gasp.

"Mama?" he croaked. "Papa?"

There was no reply. Nothing but the sound of something trickling, or pouring, maybe dripping. Splashing, perhaps. In the kitchen.

"Mama? Papa?"

He trod as quietly as he could past the door of the bedroom he shared with his brother and sister. Past his parents' room. Something told him that he needed to say nothing. That all this soundless creeping around meant nothing if he was calling out.

Yet he couldn't stop. He needed to know where his parents were. Anyone at all. This shell was far too hollow, far too empty. Nothing like a home at all. More like a tomb.

From the door that led into the kitchen, he saw light. Sickly, thin light. Barely enough of it.

And the sound. Pouring, or splashing. Or trickling. Dripping.

"Mama? Papa?"

He stepped lightly into the kitchen. Carefully. Silently.

"Mama?"

No reply.

"Papa?"

No reply.

"Nadine? Nadine!"

His sister was sitting on the floor, over by the back door. She was cradling something in her arms. Something about the size of a small child. Brown and white and red.

The puddle beside Nadine's knee was such a red, even in the weak light from the lantern in the corner. Red, and growing slowly, fed by the trickle that led from the goat's neck. Its head hung at such a strange angle, and the blood just kept trickling, dripping. Draining into the spreading puddle.

"Nadine?"

His sister looked up. Her eyes were red, and blank. Almost as blank as Iggy's.

"Nadine?" His voice barely more than an empty croak. "Nadine, what happened?"

"It's Iggy — she's sick."

"Nadine, I think . . ."

"She's sick, Scally."

Taking a deep breath. "Yes, she's very sick, Nadine."

"Will she get better? I don't think she's going to get better, do you?"

How to answer? Honestly? With a kind lie? By putting off the truth for another time? A better time? A time when someone else could explain that cut throats don't just . . .

He didn't answer. Instead, he knelt beside his sister and began to lift the goat from her arms.

"What are you doing?" She held on firmly. "Where are you taking her?"

"Nadine . . ."

Now she clung on even more tightly, and Iggy's head swung crookedly. Just the violence of that short swing made Pascal catch his breath. Like a hook caught in his chest.

Gently prying Nadine's fingers away from the dead goat's body, which was still warm. Not yet stiff, her nose still shiny and damp.

As he lifted Iggy and placed her gently to one side, Nadine began to cry. Quietly at first, but then more loudly. Wracking sobs.

Pascal took her face in his hands and looked into her eyes. Blood from the dead goat was now smeared on her cheek.

She didn't seem to notice.

"Nadine, listen. Stop crying."

He waited. She kept crying, which gave him a moment to think about what he'd seen, what might have happened and what he should do next.

He thought hard about it, but no ideas came.

"Nadine, stop crying. It's important that you listen to me."

She swallowed hard, eventually managed to stop crying. Now her breathing was ragged.

"Nadine, who did this? Who . . . did this to Iggy?"

"She's sick, Scally. I think she's sick."

He didn't want to shake his sister. He didn't want to frighten her. But then he *did* shake her, by the shoulders, and it *did* frighten her. Her eyes sprang open.

"Scally?"

"Nadine, who did this?"

"The men," Nadine replied at last. "The men came."

"Did you see them?"

Nadine shook her head. "But I heard them."

"Where were you?"

"I was hiding."

"Where?"

"Under the sheets," she said. "The big pile, in Mama's room. But I heard them. I didn't think they'd do anything to Iggy. I thought they were only looking for beetles. That's what they said."

"Beetles? Do you mean cockroaches?"

"Maybe." Her chin was crumpling again. "Oh, Iggy," she said, her eyes straying across to the goat lying there, with its head bent back strangely, its eyes blank and staring. "Scally, they killed Iggy. But she's not a beetle."

Pascal took his sister's face in his hands again. "Nadine, where are Mama and Papa? Were they here when the men came?"

Nadine nodded.

"And where are they now? Where are Mama and Papa now?"

She shrugged. "Maybe they're looking for beetles too."

Do you mind if we stop for a bit?

Of course. Like I told you at the beginning, we can stop any time. Are you all right?

I'm fine. I just want to stop for a while.

Is it upsetting to talk about this?

What do you think?

Honestly? I think it would be upsetting to talk about it.

Well it is. Kind of, I guess. It's been a few years, so . . .

But do you still remember how it felt? Even though it's been years?

Sure. I remember it well. Most of it, anyway. Some bits aren't completely clear, but others . . .

Do you remember how it felt when your parents weren't there?

Yes, that part I remember. Of course.

So how did that feel? Can you try to explain it?

I don't know. It's weird, I guess. They'd always been there before. And then they weren't. Wait, I thought we were having a break.

Sorry. I asked you a question, and you kept talking.

You tricked me into talking some more.

I wasn't tricking you.

That's how it felt.

I'm sorry I gave you that impression. I didn't mean to trick you.

It's just that sometimes people try to do that. They try to trick me.

I'm sorry.

I don't like people tricking me.

Of course. But when you're ready, I'd like to hear about —

I want to stop. I want to stop now.

We've got a little bit of time left, if you'd like to —

No. I want to stop, and I want to go. Please.

Pascal, it's just that —

You told me on Monday. You said that if I didn't want to talk I didn't have to.

That's true.

But I also said that if you didn't want to talk you could just sit there and say nothing.

I'd rather just go. I'm feeling a bit upset. It's okay — I'll still come back tomorrow.

It's not that. After what you just told me —

Really? You don't think it's always in my head anyway? Just bouncing around?

I'd rather you weren't alone.

I've spent so much time alone with this stuff over the last five years. Do you really think another twenty-four hours is going to make a difference?

I guess not . . . Where are you going?

I told you. I've had enough for today. I'll see you tomorrow.

Collège Secondaire de Saint Matthieu, **Belgium**

Come in, Pascal. Please, sit down. How are you today?

I don't know. Okay, I guess.

You look tired. And you took off quite abruptly yesterday.

I am tired.

Are you getting enough sleep?

Seriously? You're seriously asking me that?

I don't under — What are you saying?

I'm saying that of course I'm not getting enough sleep. I haven't slept properly for five years. But it's been even worse this week. And especially last night, after what we talked about.

I understand. Actually, let me reword that. I don't understand, obviously. But yesterday you'd had enough. Was it talking about what happened to your family?

What do you think?

I think that it's bringing up deep memories of terrible events.

Did you have to go to university to work that out?

Okay. Um . . . Pascal, did something happen at home last night? I want you to be completely —

Like what?

I don't know. A fight, perhaps, or . . . or something else?

Really? Because I opened that racist idiot's locker with his own head on Monday, suddenly you think I'm getting into fights all the time?

I'm sorry, Pascal, that's not what I'm suggesting at all. It's just that you've come in here looking very tired and sounding very angry, and in light of the way you left here yesterday I was simply concerned that —

Well, don't be. Okay? Don't be concerned. I'm pretty tough. Do you really think not getting enough sleep is going to be my biggest problem? After everything I've told you?

I suppose not.

That's right. So can we get started? This is the last day, right? Of . . . of *this*?

That's the general idea, yes.

Good. Then let's get on with it. Where was I?

The goat.

The goat. Yes.

Agabande, Rwanda

The noise. It went on all night. Even from Pascal and Nadine's hiding spot in the water tank, the sounds crept in. The trucks groaned by, the men shouting, chanting. "Kill the cockroaches, kill them all, don't let a single one live!"

When the trucks weren't going by, people were running past on the road. Running. Panting. Footsteps. And then, after that, the trucks would come by some more, sometimes slow, sometimes fast. Voices calling out to one another.

From time to time the rain would start again. It was welcome, too, when it did. The sound of raindrops drumming on the metal side of the tank that actually formed the roof of the hideout. It drowned out the calls and the screaming and the shouting and the popping far off in the distance.

"How long do we have to stay in here?" Nadine kept asking. At the beginning she'd asked at a normal kind of volume, but Pascal kept insisting that she only whisper. He couldn't see her, but he could feel her, huddled against him. Shivering.

And asking so many questions. Meanwhile there were so few satisfactory answers. And quite a few lies.

"Where are Mama and Papa?"

"I don't know. You said they were looking for beetles."

"The men said that Mama and Papa had to help them. Are they coming home soon?"

"Yes."

"Where's J-B?"

"At Kami's house."

"When can we go inside? I'm tired."

"Soon, I hope."

"Macaron's tired too. He needs to go to bed."

"I know. Soon."

"Who were those men who hurt Iggy, Scally? Why were they looking for bugs?"

"Because they think bugs are dirty." Dirty. It felt wrong to think of his family that way. They weren't dirty!

"Why don't they just use Jolt spray, if they want to kill bugs and beetles?"

"It doesn't work."

"Yes it does! I've seen Mama kill mosquitoes and spiders and cockroaches with it. I'm going to call those men 'Jolts.'"

"It's a good name."

"Because it's for getting rid of bugs."

"Yes, I understood what you meant. Shh, remember, not so loud."

"Sorry, Scally."

A long pause. She huddled closer. Sighed. "When can we go inside? I'm tired."

"I know. You said. *Please* don't talk so loud, okay?"

"Okay, Scally. Sorry."

"Are you thirsty?"

"A bit."

"Wait." Feeling around for the Primus beer bottle he'd filled with water just the day before. Or was it the day before that? Finding the bottle, pressing it into his sister's hand. "Here. It's water. Don't drink too much."

She drank from the bottle. Made a kind of gagging noise. "It tastes yuck."

"The bottle had beer in it."

"I don't think I like beer."

"I know. Why don't you lie down with Macaron and have a little sleep?" he suggested.

"I'm a bit cold. And hungry."

It was going to become a problem eventually anyway. Food and water. And going to the toilet, but he'd worry about that when the time came.

"Nadine, I'm going to go and get a blanket and something to eat, all right?"

"I want to come with you."

"No. Wait here."

Suddenly her voice was building in volume. "But Scally, I want to come with —"

"Shh! No, I need you to stay right here. I'll be back soon." Hoping that this wasn't one of the lies.

Poking his head out of the hole in the tank. Looking round. It was the coldest part of the night. He hadn't realized how warm they really were in the tank with their own body heat.

Checking again. The night was still and silent.

His heart thumping, Pascal scurried across to the house, let himself in the back door. Trying not to look at

Iggy's dark shape, with her impossible neck and staring eyes. Dashing into Mama and Papa's room, snatching up a blanket. Hurrying back through the kitchen, stepping over the blood on the floor. Grabbing some plantains, some bananas, a pot of cassava from the stove. Flies rose from it, and just for a moment, his thoughts went to the can of Jolt.

Back across the yard, ducking down, scrambling on his knees back into the tank.

"Scally? You were gone for ages."

"I wasn't really."

"Is Mama back yet?"

"No."

"How about Papa?"

"No. Neither is J-B. Here, eat a banana. And I got a blanket, too. You should try to sleep."

Perhaps he should sleep, too. He lay down beside his sister, pulled her head onto his shoulder. She didn't resist. And soon her breathing fell into the slow rhythm of exhausted sleep.

A burst of sound as someone charged through the back door of the house. Their footsteps came across the lawn and towards the water tank. They were panting. Panting and sobbing. Perhaps praying, too. They were saying something. "Please, please, please ..." Or words very much like that.

The footsteps went past the tank and stopped somewhere behind the chicken house. The sound of panting, the sound of sobbing continued. The sound of a terrified person trying to calm themselves down so that their breathing wouldn't give them away. They weren't doing a very good job.

The back door bursting open again. This person not even trying to remain quiet.

The voice not loud, but menacing. Terrifying. Smiling. "I know you're out here, cockroach. You can't run away forever. I will find you. I don't care what rock you crawled under, I will find you."

The menacing voice coming closer. Pascal holding his own breath, squeezing Nadine's hand, urging her with his mind to keep quiet. Her eyes shining and wide in the deep dimness. She was learning.

Nadine's name for the bad men was perfect. Jolts. "Cockroach . . . Cockroach . . . Cockroach . . ." The singsong voice coming much, much closer. Footsteps stopping by the tank. The toes of one bare foot visible through the hole. "Come on, cockroach. I know you're out here somewhere."

Don't look down here, Pascal thought. He prayed it. *Please, God. Please, Jesus. Please, Mother Mary. Please don't let him look down here.*

"What are you hiding from?" the voice asked. "I don't want to hurt you. I just want to talk to you."

Please, Mother Mary.

"I can hear you. I can hear your breathing."

Whose breathing could the Jolt hear? Pascal's? Nadine's? The terrified person behind the chicken shed?

Please, Jesus.

The footsteps moving away now. Away from the tank. Towards the chicken shed. The sound of the gate to the chicken run being lifted aside. Chickens stirring, grumbling in their funny little voices.

"Well now, this is a lovely little hidey-hole, isn't it?" the Jolt said. "Just perfect for a cockroach. Except . . . wait, chickens eat insects and grubs and cockroaches, don't they?"

The door of the chicken shed itself being opened. The sudden disturbance of the chickens swelled and flared like a panic. Flapping, squawking, screaming, shouting.

"You idiot," the Jolt was saying. Laughing. Laughter with an angry edge. "Maybe you're not a cockroach — at least they know how to hide."

"Please, don't hurt me!" the woman begged. Her voice rising above the angry squawks of the frightened birds, then falling in amongst them like someone being pulled under by a mob.

"I told you to come out quietly, but you didn't, did you?"

"I'm sorry! Please, I have a child!"

"You have a child? Where?"

"What?"

"*Where* is your child?"

"Wait! No, I don't have children! I have no children! If you have to kill me, just do it, but don't hurt my . . . I don't have any kids!"

"Which is it?" the Jolt asked. "Do you or don't you have children?"

"I don't."

"So there's no one to miss you, is there?"

"Um . . ."

"Is there?"

187

"Wait . . ."

"Too slow. Too late. We'll find your kid one way or another."

A scream. Then another, almost drowned out by the screaming chickens. Angry words that Pascal couldn't quite understand from the Jolt. A third scream, long and loud, piercing the night. Then a heavy thump, a thud with a sharp edge to the sound, and the scream stopped. Instantly. Stopped. Stopped dead.

"You should have come out when I told you," the Jolt said. Pascal heard him spit. "All the cockroaches who are hiding should just come out and get it over with."

Pascal wondering, is he talking to me? Me and Nadine? Does he know we're here? Or is it a general warning for any people hidden in the garden, or in the shadows amongst the trees?

The sound of a truck engine, the sound of a horn.

"Coming," the Jolt called. "I'm done here."

Footsteps drifting away.

Sometime after the Jolt left, Pascal heard the cry. A tiny, mewling cry, almost like a kitten.

"It's a baby," Nadine said. It was the first thing she'd said since the commotion in the chicken shed.

"I don't think so."

"It is. My friend Claudette has a baby sister. It sounds just like that."

The woman had a child. She'd blurted it out, then tried to cover it up. But she'd said it.

"Stay here."

"I could come and help you with the —"

"No! No, you and Macaron stay here."

Once again crawling out into the wet grass. Checking carefully that he wasn't joining someone in the garden.

It was almost dawn. The sky was paler now, and the rain had made everything seem cleaner, somehow. The chickens were wandering around the yard, lifting their feet high, as if they couldn't quite understand how they had come to be out while it was still nighttime. He didn't go into the chicken shed with the smashed gate. Maybe if he couldn't find the baby anywhere else he'd have to check. But for now, he didn't want to see what he knew was in there.

The mewling led him around the side of the hideout to the stand that the good tank perched on. There, partly obscured by a large tuft of grass, he found the baby. Uncovered, damp, its mouth moving as if in search of milk. Its tiny fingers opening, closing, opening some more, as if it was trying to grasp something out of the thin air.

He picked up the baby, and for a moment, the way its head fell back reminded him of Iggy.

Pascal hurried around to the entrance to the hideout and crouched down. "Here, Nadine. I found it. Can you help me look after it?"

"A baby? What's its name?"

"I think it's just called Baby."

"And where's its mama?"

Time for one more lie.

"I don't know."

Baby was quiet now. After he'd wrapped it in the end of the blanket, it had kept making the kitten-like noise for a while. But then it had stopped. Then some more mewling for a while, and it stopped again. Bit by bit the quiet periods grew longer than the crying periods. When it did cry, Pascal tried something that he'd seen ladies with little babies do in church. He put the tip of his finger in Baby's warm mouth, and it sucked weakly for a while. When he held it to his cheek, he felt the warm breath. Weak, but warm.

After a while, he gave Nadine the job of providing a fingertip. It made her feel useful, he guessed, and she was keen for a while. But eventually she got more tired as well, and eventually fell asleep once more. Her breathing steady and slow and deep. So tired.

Pascal was tired too. So tired. He wasn't sure how long they'd been in the tank now, except that the grass outside the hole in the tank was brighter now. More light. Morning was arriving.

But he couldn't let himself sleep. Not while he had Nadine and Baby to look after.

He heard the now familiar sound of one of the trucks groaning slowly by, gears crunching and brakes squealing. He heard the music. Tinny, too loud, making the speakers buzz. He heard the Jolts riding on the truck, banging their machetes and clubs on the metal floor in time with their chanting.

"Kill the roaches, kill them all. Don't leave a single one behind."

Pascal placed his hand near Baby's face, ready to clamp

it down over her mouth if she was woken by the Jolts on the truck. If she began to cry. There was no warm breath now. There was no warm breath coming from Baby's mouth, and when Pascal rested his hand gently on Baby's face, it was cold. Not icy cold, just clammy. Like a piece of meat.

The truck was farther away now, and Pascal took a deep breath. He sucked it in with much more force than he meant to, and the sound surprised him as it echoed around the tank. This sound wasn't just a breath — it was a cry.

His sudden sob woke Nadine. She whimpered.

"Shh," Pascal said. He wiped the tears from his cheek with the back of his hand. Even in the dark, he felt ashamed of crying. He had to be the big boy. Time to grow up.

"Scally?"

"Shh."

"Scally? Is Baby all right?"

"No."

"What happened? Did the Jolts get her like they got Iggy?"

How to answer? There was no blood. No head hanging at a terrible angle. But the correct answer to Nadine's question was still yes.

"No," he said. "She just got too tired, I think."

"Oh," Nadine said. "Shame."

"Yes. Shame." Barely keeping his voice steady.

His blood ran cold as he heard footsteps crunching in the gravel at the end of the path that led from the house. Without a second thought he clamped his hand over Nadine's mouth.

"I'll check out here," said a voice that Pascal thought he recognized. It took him a moment, but then he got it.

It was Henri's father.

"I'll catch up," Pascal heard Henri's father say. "I just need to use the toilet."

"Go pee behind a tree like the rest of us," another of the men replied.

"It's not a pee that I need to do," the Jolt answered.

"Ah! Well, don't get lost. And don't step in anything." A laugh.

"I won't. I'll find you."

"Stay safe." The other Jolt laughed.

"I think I'll be all right. After all, I've got this." A metallic scrape, a machete tip against the concrete of the old tank stand.

Footsteps were coming closer across the yard. Soft, padding footsteps.

Pascal held his breath. The footsteps came all the way up to the tank and stopped. Through the gap between the two panels, Pascal saw the man's feet. His shoes. White Adidas, three green stripes. Red laces. And beside the man's feet the blade of a machete, dark rusty red stains along its length, its tip resting lightly in the damp grass.

"I know you're in there," the Jolt suddenly said, his voice little more than a murmur. "And I know who you are."

Pascal holding his breath.

"I know you're in there, and I know who you're in there with."

Still holding his breath.

192

"I'm sorry for what you've seen. And for the goat."

Struggling to hold his breath much longer. Feeling another sob growing in the centre of the chest. Feeling his eyes prick with tears as he remembered Iggy's head lolling wrongly, and his sister not understanding.

"I'm sorry about the goat, but not for your parents. Wait, I mean . . . Your parents are still alive. I think. For now."

The Jolt's voice stopped as a truck drove slowly by the front of the house, its springs creaking and thumping on the rough, rutted road. Chanting, shouting, whooping.

Then the truck was gone.

Pascal heard the sound of liquid spattering on the ground. A thin stream of yellow between the shoes. White Adidas with three green stripes on each side. And on the left shoe, a red-rust smudge across the toe.

"Listen," the man murmured as the stream of pee continued. "Don't say anything. Don't come out. Not for anything. If you do come out, there's nothing I can do to help you. Nothing, do you understand? So stay there. For my son's sake, if nothing else."

The stream of yellow had turned into a dribble, then stopped. Pascal saw that some of the pee had splashed on one of his father's shoes. He felt a surge of anger as he remembered how his father wiped over those shoes and placed them safely away in their box every Sunday evening.

Now the feet were gone.

"Who was that man?" Nadine asked.

"Shh."

"What did he want?"

"Shh."

"I have to go to the toilet."

"I told you not to drink too much water."

"I didn't!"

"All right, keep your voice down."

Then came the sound he least expected, rolling in from across the valley. Around their house and drifting into their dark hideout.

"Is that the church bell?" Nadine asked.

"I think so." Listening. "Yes, it is."

"Why are they ringing the bell? Is it Sunday?"

He had to think. It was Friday, wasn't it? "I don't think it's Sunday."

"But they only ring the bell on Sunday, don't they? Remember, it's J-B's job."

"I remember."

"So it must be Sunday."

Maybe she was right. Perhaps they'd spent much longer in the tank than he'd realized.

It was definitely the bell. The church bell. A place of refuge, Father Michel had said.

A decision. The right one? Perhaps, perhaps not. How could he know?

Henri's father had told him to stay. A thief and a goat-murderer.

Father Michel had said that the church was a safe place.

There would be food in that safe place. Food, and water that didn't taste like beer. And maybe his family. All the way over the other side of the valley.

"Nadine. Listen. We're going to go to church."

"Are Mama and Papa there?"

"I think we should find out, don't you?"

"Should we take Baby with us?" Nadine asked.

"No. We'll leave Baby here. We can't help Baby any more."

"Oh. Shame."

"Yes. Shame. Wait here," he ordered.

"Where are you going?"

"Just outside for a second."

Glancing around. No one in sight. Everything quiet, even the dogs. Only the birds in the undergrowth made any kind of sound.

Sneaking through the house. More light only showed Iggy's body in more detail, and he had to hold back, force himself not to vomit. He was so hungry.

To the front door, past his father's carvings of gorillas and chimps and birds. Standing well inside the door, poking his head around the post.

In that moment, he actually doubted his own eyes. Blinked. Squinted. Had to wrestle with his stomach once more.

Bodies. Some lying on the road, face down. Some lying on their backs, their arms and legs in all sorts of unnatural positions. Some slumped against walls and fences. Some still moving, barely.

What had happened out here?

And then he did vomit.

And the bell kept ringing.

Pascal crouched down at the entrance to the tank. "Okay," he said. "We need to hurry. But listen, Nadine. I want you to do something, and you have to promise me that you'll do it. Do you promise?"

"You haven't said what it is yet."

"I know, but I will. But you have to promise. Okay?"

Nadine nodded.

"I want you to hang on to the back of my shirt and only look down."

"Why?"

"Because I don't want you to look around."

"Why not?"

How to explain? How to tell her about the bodies and the faces and the blood and the . . . the sheer *awfulness* of what was scattered about them?

And the silence. That was what he worried about most for his sister — that she would hear nothing and wonder why, and look up and around. And then she'd see . . .

"Just trust me, okay? It's really important."

"Okay, Scally. I will."

"You'll hang on to my shirt? And not let go?"

"I promise."

"And not look up?"

"I promise."

"Unless I tell you to look up."

"What?"

He needed to ready her for the possibility that at some point he might need to grab her hand and shout, "Run!" But how to prepare her for that?

"Just hang on to the back of my shirt and don't let go. Now, it's quite a long way."

"Where are we going?" Nadine asked.

"To the church, remember?"

Nadine's volume was beginning to rise. "But that's all the way over the other side of the town and up the hill!"

"Shh! Shush, Nadine! So it's a bit of a walk, but we have to go. Now. All right? You *have* to trust me."

"Can Baby come?"

"No. Baby needs to stay here so her mama can find her."

"That makes sense. How about Iggy?"

"No, we talked about that before and . . . Do you have Macaron?"

"Yes," she said, holding her doll high.

"Good. Then we have everything we need. Come on, it's time to go. And remember, hang on tight and don't look around."

Suddenly Nadine brightened. A realization! "Is this a game, like hide-and-seek?"

A great idea. Why hadn't he thought of that?

"Yes. It's exactly like that. It's a special kind of hide-and-seek, where you count to . . . How high can you count?"

"One . . . two . . . three . . . four . . . five . . ."

"Okay, good. Just keep doing that. I'll tell you when it's time to stop counting. Have you got hold of my shirt? All right, then let's go."

At the beginning, Pascal kept checking that his sister wasn't looking around. He could feel her grip on his shirt, and he could sense that her footsteps were faltering at times.

But then, as they reached the end of their road, he felt her grip loosen, just a little. Then it tightened again, and finally it pulled hard against him as she stopped.

Even before he turned back to check, he knew that she was looking around. And when he did turn back, he saw her eyes as wide as he'd ever seen them. Her expression was one of proper disbelief.

He remembered that feeling; he'd had it less than half an hour ago. He wondered if his face had been as blank as hers was now. Of course it had been.

"Scally . . ."

"I told you not to look!" Completely angry, not that she'd disobeyed him, but because he could no longer protect her from what was all around them. All those bodies, lying, slumped, scattered alone and piled together.

"I couldn't help it." Nadine's voice far more calm than he might have expected. "I looked up by accident. Scally, are all these people dead?"

"Yes."

"Like Iggy?"

"Yes."

"And Baby? Is Baby dead too?"

"Yes."

"Are Mama and Papa dead too, Scally?"

He *could* say no. No, they're not dead. They'll be back soon. But he didn't know that. In fact, since he'd seen what was in the streets, in the gardens, in the grass beside the roads, he doubted that they would be back at all. Ever.

"They're fine. They'll be fine."

"So they might be all right?"

"Yes. Come on, we're wasting time," he said as the bell began to ring once more. "We're going to be late for Mass."

"Maybe Mama and Papa are waiting at the church for us," Nadine suggested.

"Maybe."

When he first said it, it was simply something to say, something that might keep his sister's hopes up. After all, she was only five. Barely five. But then, as he agreed with her just to keep her calm, he found himself wondering if she was right. Perhaps that was exactly where his parents were, waiting for their kids at the top of the hill with wide smiles and open arms. He pushed down the thought that they wouldn't have gone to the church first, but would have come straight home to check on their children. But that was an inconvenient thought. A thought he didn't like one bit.

"Someone's ringing the bell again," Nadine said. "Is that J-B?"

"Maybe."

"I can't wait to see him. And Mama and Papa. But not Tee-bee. He won't be there, because he lives in Bell-jum."

"That's true." Because it was true. Taribe did live in Belgium, and in that moment Pascal imagined his eldest brother being given the news. He didn't know how bad news was delivered in Belgium. Someone walking into your house when you weren't expecting them? A phone call? A police officer knocking on the front door, perhaps. But none of that mattered, because in that moment of imagining Taribe getting the bad news, the method by which he'd been told that news completely disappeared. All he could see was his brother's eyes, wide and disbelieving. Unable to comprehend that his entire family had been wiped out. Murdered in their little town, right across the valley from the church and the seminary. Something truly impossible to believe.

No, he couldn't let himself think that way. He didn't even know if it were true.

And yet Pascal and his sister were walking through it. Right through the middle of it. Bodies and destruction, a few houses still smoking from where their windows had been smashed and burning tires thrown in. The silence was pierced only by the ringing of the bell, and the occasional cry or whimper from the street, or the drains beside the road, from within houses.

With almost every step, Pascal listened hard for the sound of more Jolts, either on foot or in their trucks, and planned an escape route. Between those two buildings there, over this overgrown bank here, away behind those trees just over the way.

"Come on, we have to hurry," he said to his sister for what felt like the hundredth time. "Jean-Baptiste's still waiting."

He thought about taking the road. It was the easiest way to go. After all, it was a road. Many, many people used it every day.

But something else now used that road. The trucks, and the Jolts.

So instead, he decided to take a different way. The shortcut that would bring them out near Mr. Ingabire's shop. The path that ran through the cool, damp forest that wrapped around the side of the hill. He knew that path. He knew spaces to hide if that became necessary.

Just before they descended into the forest, he looked across the valley towards the church. People were climbing the path, drawn by the ringing bell. Hurrying, it seemed. As if the service couldn't start until they arrived. Not dressed in white, but in their normal, everyday clothes.

Pascal and his sister set out along the path through the forest, but they had taken barely a hundred steps when Nadine stopped, and began tugging on his sleeve.

He shrugged his arm free. "What?"

She was whispering. "I found someone."

"What are you talking about?"

"Hide-and-seek. Look." She pointed into the forest, and Pascal followed her finger.

Down there, in the dark, cool spaces between the bread-fruit trees and vines, were more splashes of colour. Human colours, the kind more often found in clothes than in nature. They were the shirts, skirts, dresses, trousers of people who had been chased into those dark, cool spaces only to discover that there was nowhere else to run. And then the yellows, oranges, blues of their clothes and the black and dark brown of their skin had been taken over by a dark, rust red. It seemed that even that less worn path hadn't been left unexplored by the Jolts.

"They're on our side," he told her. "We have to let them keep on hiding."

Nadine screwed up her nose. "I thought we were . . . This

is a silly game of hide-and-seek. Do you even know how to play?"

"This is a special way of playing, with very special rules," he told her.

"I've never heard of it."

"That's because you have to be five to know the special rules, and you are five now, so . . ."

Suddenly brightening. "This is like my game! And J-B's game! You know — mine's called the People Game, with people in the leaves. And J-B's game is called the Chasing Game, where people have to run away!"

"Maybe," Pascal said, a bottomless pit of exhaustion opening beneath him. How much longer could he do this? Keep telling lies and half-truths to his sister just so she would keep up?

"I think that's what they're playing," she was saying.

"I think you're right. So maybe we should leave them to play it, okay? Come on, we've still got a way to go."

"What's that smell?"

"I know."

"Pascal, I'm tired."

"So am I. Just keep up."

"And thirsty."

"Later."

The bell was still ringing. But for how much longer? Would it stop ringing soon, and when it did, would it mean that the church was full? That no one else could take shelter there?

Another horrible thought. His mother and father

hugging one another and staring out as the church door was closed. Staring out, hoping to see Pascal and Nadine come into view at the top of the hill. And the door closing completely. No one else allowed in. No more room.

They reached the street that ran behind the line of shops and up through the open-air market. Pulling his sister down beside him, Pascal crouched behind one of the small hut-like market stalls that were built right up to the edge of the rutted road. He listened for voices, or the sounds of trucks or motorbikes. Signs of life. There were none. Not close by, at least — somewhere far off he heard a motorcycle engine. But close by, it was practically silent.

He poked his head out. The market was quiet, even for a Sunday. A few dogs sniffed around some of the piles of clothes that had been left lying in the red mud, and farther up the hill a few figures moved about amongst the piles. Slowly. From one to the next, sometimes shooing the dogs away, sometimes stopping long enough to bring their sticks or machetes down on the bundles of rags, like the women who beat the suds out of their washing down by the town pump.

Except these weren't just piles of clothes they were beating. Pascal knew that they were just like the splashes of colour he'd seen in the undergrowth farther up the shortcut path. Fabrics that had once been colourful, then faded with time, and now stained with the same rusty red.

"Come on," he said to Nadine. "We're going over there." Pointing towards the narrow gap between Mr. Ingabire's shop and the clinic. More bodies in that gap. He didn't want to get too close to them, but there was no way around it. Not if they wanted to get over the main street and up to the church.

The Singhs' clinic van wasn't parked in its usual place behind the clinic. But worse than that, the back door of the building had been kicked in, windows smashed. Three or four lengths of bandage hung from one of the broken windows. Whoever had ransacked the place for bandages wasn't using them on the people lying in the street.

"Quickly." Pascal took Nadine's hand, gave a quick glance in both directions, then darted across the road and into the gap. Keeping himself between his sister and the bodies. Shielding her eyes.

The next stage of the journey. To cross the main road. To the strangler fig, perhaps to find a spot in the folds of its roots and the vines engulfing its enormous base.

"Nadine," he said. "Remember how I said we were playing a special kind of hide-and-seek?"

She looked at him like he was crazy. Of course she remembered.

"So, this is the next part. We have to go over to that tree. But we have to run. No stopping and looking around. Okay?"

"Okay."

A quick check, up and down the street. Like the market, this street was strangely empty. At one of the crossroads in the direction of the tourist lodge a truck crossed the main street. Men were packed into the back. Other men jogged alongside.

The sound of their chanting drifted to Pascal, past the

figures who were wandering the main street and, like those in the market, moving from one pile of rust-stained clothes to the next.

No. He had to stop thinking that they were simply bundles of fabric. They were *bodies*. He had to accept it. Dead bodies. People who had died. Been killed.

"You!" A deep voice. "Come out and stop sneaking around."

Mr. Ingabire had been sweeping his front step, fighting a battle with the red dust, which was now red mud. And being mud, it simply refused to be swept anywhere. But now he had something else to grab his attention.

"Oh, it's you again! And your little sister. Where are your parents? You probably shouldn't be out. Not in all . . . this." A sweep of the hand. So casual as he indicated the bodies, crooked, crumpled, spread about. "It's no place for kids. Maybe you should go home and wait for this to blow over." He glanced up at the overcast sky, as if what was happening all around them was, in fact, nothing more than a passing rainstorm. "Where did you say your parents were?"

"We think they're up at the church," Nadine said. "My brother rings the bell, you know."

"Does he?" The briefest of half-smiles. "Well, I hope he's —" Mr. Ingabire suddenly stopped talking, reached inside the doorway and turned up the radio.

". . . reports that some forces are trying to fight back," the announcer was saying. "Our numbers are much greater, and resistance has been a lot lighter than we expected, proving once again that the enemy is not simply small in number, but small in courage as well. Even so, don't be fooled. Don't go soft now. Just remember the cockroaches under the bin. You can't leave even one."

Mr. Ingabire clicked off the radio.

"So where are you going, then?"

"Nowhere," Pascal said.

"Didn't you say the church? I think that's probably wise. It's safer, you see."

"You should come with us," Nadine said to him. "Mama says that you should close your shop and go to church on Sunday. She says that you're going to hell because you don't go to church on Sunday."

"*Does* she?" he said. "Well, isn't that nice? So, off you go, then. Up the hill to church. You can't be late. Say hi to your parents for me, especially your mother. Tell her I'll think about coming to church sometime."

"Come on," Pascal said, grabbing Nadine's arm. Something about Mr. Ingabire's tone troubled him.

"Are we still playing hide-and-seek in the big tree?" she asked.

"No. We're going straight up to the church."

"But I wanted to play hide-and-seek!"

"I don't think there's a lot of time," Mr. Ingabire said. "You should get going. Don't stop for anything. They're waiting for you."

Another truck came around the corner up by the motorbike mechanic's shop and drove slowly along the street towards their corner. Slowly, and full of men. They waved sticks, heavy beams of wood. Some had machetes. Jolts. They had to be.

"Look!" Nadine said, pointing as the truck picked its way around the bodies on the road. "Are they the men that killed —"

"Go," Mr. Ingabire said to Pascal. "Go now. I'll talk to these ones."

Pascal didn't need to be told again. He took Nadine's hand and jogged across the road. As they ran under the huge canopy of the strangler fig he looked up. Up there, too? Not just in the ditches and the gutters and the undergrowth and the houses and the laneways and alleys and the streets, but in the branches of a huge tree? What was he seeing? It was like a terrible dream, only worse. At least in a dream you could sometimes remind yourself that it wasn't real. That you could wake up from it. And then you would.

But not this. Bodies hanging from branches, or tucked away in the folds of the huge buttress roots as if they were just taking a nap. Except . . . His eyes saw it, but he didn't want to trust them. The hands. In some cases the feet.

"Not the main road," he said, more to himself than to his sister. "We'll cut up through the plantain garden. That way we'll go past Henri's house."

"He doesn't go to church," Nadine pointed out. "He's going to go to hell like Mr. Ingabire."

Heaven or hell — it must be busy at the pearly gates today.

"Don't say that," he said to Nadine.

She was already on to the next subject. "I'm hungry."

Hungry. Yes, and so was he. He wished she hadn't said that, hadn't reminded him that he hadn't eaten anything for . . . how long?

"Can I eat some cassava?"

"No! It has to be cooked." Didn't it? Or was that some kind of old wives' tale?

"Just the leaves. I'm really hungry, Scally!"

"No, it's poisonous." Probably. It was hard to think straight.

"Just the leaves, I said!"

"No, it's *all* poisonous. They'll have food at the church."

He didn't know if this was true. But now his sister wasn't just tired, but hungry too. He needed something to keep her moving.

"What sort of food will they have?"

"I'll tell you while we walk."

Up the hill, trying to stay away from the exposed places. Then the rain, beginning to fall all over again. Now walking up the hill had turned into slipping over in the mud on the hill.

"Scally?"

"Shush. I know it's raining, and I know you're tired. We're nearly there." Kind of true. True enough.

"No. Scally, where did the hands go?"

"What are you talking about?"

"The people under the tree. Where did their hands go?"

The hands. The feet. All gone.

"I don't know. I think someone cut them off." Coming up with new lies, new explanations was exhausting.

"Will the hands and feet come back?"

Feeling a sudden rush of fury. Not at the Jolts — the confusion and rage he felt towards them was still too deep to even drag out into the light. No, anger at his sister for being so young, so stupid, asking such dumb questions.

Turning to face her. Grabbing her shoulders. Shaking her. Shouting. "Enough questions, Nadine! All right? How can hands and feet come back?"

His sister's head snapping back and forth like her neck was a piece of string. Her ridiculous doll at the end of her arm, its head snapping back and forth as he shook Nadine hard enough to hurt her.

"Tell me!" he shouted. "How?"

Nadine trying to pull herself free, succeeding, but then overbalancing on the muddy slope and falling. Tumbling like a toy, turning over three times, landing hard, face down.

She didn't move. Not at first. She just lay there in the mud, her forehead resting in the bend of her elbow. Pascal saw her back shaking. She was crying. Of course she was crying. He felt like crying himself, and *he* hadn't just fallen down a steep hill and landed in the mud.

"Nadine, I'm sorry." He scrambled down to where she lay. She tried to pull away again as he began to turn her over. He gripped her harder. Turned her over at last.

Pretty much all of her front side was covered in mud. Her dress, her face, everything.

"I'm sorry."

"Why were you angry, Scally?"

Where to begin?

"Look. That's Henri's house up there." Pointing through a gap in the plantain leaves. The red mud house with the timber roof. The windows seemed to be frowning down at them. Daring them to come closer.

"Maybe they have some food they can give us," Nadine suggested.

"Yes, maybe they do. I'll go and find out. Wait here. Don't move." Pascal pointed at the ground. "Right here, okay?"

"Where are you going, Scally?"

"I'm just going to see if Henri's home."

"Why can't I come with you?"

"Just . . . " Biting down on the frustration at having to explain everything to his little sister. "Please, just wait here like I said. All right?"

"I don't want to be by myself."

"You won't be. You've got Macaron. I'll be back as soon as —"

Stopped mid-sentence by a scream from Nadine.

"Stop screaming! What's wrong?"

"Macaron! I don't have Macaron!"

"What do you mean, you don't have him? Where is he?"

His sister was turning in small, desperate circles, looking on the ground, under her feet, at her hands . . .

"Nadine! Where's Macaron?"

"I don't know!" Wailing. *"I . . . don't . . . know!"*

Think. Think *hard*. Where could that stupid doll be?

"When did you have it last?"

"Wha . . . what?"

Suddenly remembering. When he was shaking her, just before she fell down the hill into the mud. He didn't like remembering the shaking and the falling, because he'd seen a cruelty in himself that he didn't like. But he liked it even less when he realized that his actions had led to that ridiculous sock-doll flying off into the plantain trees and cassava stalks.

"It's gone," he said. "He's gone. I'm sorry."

"Where is he?"

He knew, and at the same time he didn't know. He knew that the doll was somewhere *down there, farther down the hill.* But could he have walked to the exact spot where it lay? Of course not. And there was no time to try. He'd have to come up with something to calm Nadine. And he'd have to come up with it quickly.

"You're going to have to stop crying," he said. "It's important."

"But Macaron —"

"Listen. Do you want to see Mama and Papa?"

Nodding. Sniffing.

"Good. Then you have to stop crying. After we've been to find Mama and Papa, then we can come back for Macaron. All right?"

"Why can't we look for him now?"

"I just told you." Even though he hadn't. "It's important that we find Mama and Papa first. Macaron will be fine."

"How do you know?"

Because he's nothing but a sock stuffed with dried grass, Pascal thought. "I just do. He's fine. He's just waiting for you quietly. Okay? Can you stop crying and wait here for me like I asked?"

Nodding and sniffing some more. But crying less now.

"Okay. Good. Stay here."

Setting out up the hill towards Henri's house. While they'd been climbing, they'd kept warm. But now, after stopping and arguing about Macaron, his wet shirt clung to his skin and chilled him through.

As Pascal approached the house, he crouched, moved more slowly. Closer now, up to a pile of wood behind the house. Looking around for signs of life. Or signs of death. None of either. It was just a house, red mud brick, timber roof. He allowed himself to breathe, catch his breath as he sank down behind the woodpile.

The church bell had been silent for a while, but now it started again. The sound spurred him on, made him stand up and scamper over to the house. He just had to check that Henri was okay. It wouldn't take very long.

He raised his head to peer over the windowsill. It would be empty in there.

Except it wasn't. Henri was sitting on his low bed, with his back to the window. Sitting quietly, with one of his knees raised as he did something with one of his feet, which was hidden from view by his body.

Whispering. "Henri. *Psst!*"

Henri turned suddenly, as if a wasp had stung him on the neck. "Hey! What's going on? I haven't seen you for days!"

"Can I come in? Wait. . ." Stopping, as Henri twisted a little more, and Pascal saw. Henri wore a shoe on his right foot. A shoe that was too large for him. A white sports shoe, with three green stripes on the side.

"Hey, do you know how to tie shoelaces?" Henri asked.

"Those shoes . . ."

"They're my dad's," Henri said. "But please don't tell him I tried them on. He'll be angry. I just wanted to see what they felt like. But I'll take them off — just don't tell him." He began yanking at the tangle of a knot that he'd tied, but that was only making it worse.

"They're nice shoes," Pascal said. "Where did he get them?"

"I don't know. How should I know?"

A decision needed to be made. To tell, or not? How could he even be sure that these white and green Adidas shoes were the ones his own father wore so proudly on Sundays? The ones he put away in the box every Sunday evening?

"Where's your dad?" Pascal asked.

"I don't know. He's been gone for ages." Finally Henri had managed to get the laces untied. He pulled the shoe off and placed it on the floor with the other one. "Promise you won't tell my dad that I was wearing his new shoes?"

"I won't tell."

"Thanks. So, what are you doing here?"

"I'm just going . . ." He stopped. Thought. Decided to lie. He wasn't even sure why — it just felt like the right thing to do. The right thing? The *best* thing. Right and best weren't always the same. "I'm just going home."

"Have you seen?" Henri asked. "Down in the town?"

"You mean all the people?"

Henri looked at the floor. Nodded.

"Yes, I've seen them."

"Cockroaches. They asked for it, you know. The guy on the radio has been saying that —"

"I've got to go. Home. I'm going home."

213

"I could come with you."

"No. Mama said I couldn't bring you with me today. That's what she said. 'Come straight home and don't bring anyone.'" I asked if you could come for lunch but she said no."

"Why not?"

"I don't know — she didn't say."

"Okay. I guess I'll see you at school tomorrow. Enjoy your lunch."

Back past the pile of wood at the edge of the hill, down the slope. It had stopped raining, but the grass and the mud were slippery, and Pascal slid a lot of the way on his butt.

"Nadine!" he called. "Come on, Nadine, we have to get up to the church!"

But when he reached the place he'd left her, she wasn't there. She'd lost her stupid sock doll, and now he'd lost her.

"Nadine? Where are you?" He turned in circles, his eyes darting around. Between the plantain trees, into the long grass, even up in the taller trees.

He stumbled farther down the hill. He wasn't angry with his sister any more — now he was totally worried.

"Nadine?" Careful not to call out too loudly. The last thing he wanted to do was alert some of the Jolts to his presence.

She wasn't there.

Maybe she'd grown bored of waiting and wandered off. At the top of the hill the church bell was still ringing.

Perhaps that was where she'd gone. Perhaps she was already at the church.

Ordinarily, the rest of the climb to the church would have been quite easy. But today, hungry, cold and frightened, Pascal found it completely exhausting. And slow.

He stayed off the road. There wasn't a lot of traffic. Mostly it was people climbing the hill. Small groups, hurrying towards the church. Hurrying towards the place where they could hide. Be safe. Perhaps be offered something to eat. Glancing back as they hurried, glancing back at the town and the hills dotted with the dead and dying.

Almost there now. Keeping an eye out for his sister. Stupid girl! He'd told her to stay there. Don't go anywhere! But she'd gone.

This was silly, struggling and slipping and fighting through undergrowth and tall grass and mud while a few steps away was a perfectly good road. Maybe he'd be better off just joining those others who were walking on that perfectly good road.

"Don't go." It wasn't really a call for help. More like a croak. "Please, don't go."

The man was lying on his back in the ditch. Pascal had almost stood on him as he'd changed course and begun to head for the road. But there he was, one arm moving weakly as he tried to get Pascal's attention, the other arm twisted under him in a way that looked completely unnatural. His knees were bent and moving back and forth, back and forth, as if he was trying to rock back and forth, ready to spring to his feet. But there'd be no springing to his feet. Blood soaked his shirt, and a gash ran across the side of his forehead and down to somewhere behind his ear. Clean edges, gaping, a hint of bony white in the middle. His mouth was full of blood, some of his teeth missing.

"Don't go."

Pascal stood over the man. Don't go? But what could he do? If he'd had to count the number of bodies he'd seen today who looked like this man — and worse — he'd have been running out of numbers he knew. How could he possibly help?

Perhaps he could wait. The man was begging him not to go. The man was dying. Maybe that was all Pascal could do — to wait with the man until he died. But that could take hours.

"I'm sorry," he said. "My sister . . ."

"Up there . . ." the man said, rolling his eyes slowly in the direction of the top of the hill.

"She's up there? You saw her? Thank you." He took a step towards the road, but then he stopped. He couldn't just walk away from the dying man.

But he had to.

"I'm sorry," he said again.

"Don't go."

"I have to. I hope you . . . get better . . ." he added, pathetically. That man wasn't ever getting better. That man was never going to leave that ditch.

No, that man would die with rain in his eyes, blood in his mouth and the sound of the church bell ringing in his ears.

In the end, Pascal didn't go to the road. He didn't join the others as they scurried along, some carrying bundles of clothing, bags, children. Scurrying towards the church and its walls of safety. In the end, he veered back towards the undergrowth and trees, and continued that way. If Nadine had gone to the road, she'd be safe. She'd probably have found someone she knew. She was a chatty, popular little thing — someone from church would have taken her by the hand. But if she hadn't gone to the road, she'd be scrambling and struggling through the same mud Pascal was struggling through, and might need help. All Pascal felt like doing was lying down and having a rest, so his little sister had to be feeling just as exhausted. Which meant that she might have been anywhere between here and the top of the hill.

He didn't find her as he climbed, not towards the gate, but towards the side of the church, on the opposite side from the seminary. From across the yard, he saw Father Oscar. He was beneath the little roof that protected the church bell from the rain, pulling the rope with one hand while his crooked, claw-like hand hung by his side. Glancing around from time to time, but not meeting the gaze of the people coming through the gate.

Something wasn't right.

Pascal made his way up to the side of the church, stopped behind the trunk of the mango tree. The rain gathered amongst the leaves and became large, heavy drops falling about him.

Listening for church-like sounds. Singing, perhaps. Maybe the sound of Father Michel preaching.

But no. The bell — that was all. The bell, the raindrops and the anxious footsteps on the muddy road.

And no Nadine. Unless she was already inside. Unless she'd made it. Unless she was inside with Mama and Papa now.

The groups of people coming to the church were thinning out now. They were still hurrying, but Pascal could see their relief as they realized that they'd made it. Some hugged as they reached the front door.

There was Father Michel now. He was at the door, welcoming the new arrivals. Showing them where they could leave their belongings. A pile was forming, made up of bags, clothes, even prized mats or smaller pieces of furniture. A growing pile.

"Come in," he was saying. "Come in, it's safe. I know, it's terrible, isn't it? So dreadful. Unbelievable. Yes, yes, come in, all of you. There's still plenty of room."

Another look at Father Oscar. His head low as he pulled down on the bell rope.

Something was definitely wrong.

"Father Oscar!" Calling out, hoping to get the young priest to notice him without drawing too much attention to himself.

No response. Not looking up.

Pascal took a step closer, then stopped uncertainly, moved back to his place behind the tree.

Calling out again, a little more than a normal voice, a little less than a shout. "Father Oscar."

It was Father Michel who heard him, turned to see who had called out. Saw him. There was a moment of confusion, as if he half-recognized Pascal, but wasn't sure where from.

Pascal stepped farther behind the tree, drawing back, trying to make himself smaller.

He heard footsteps in the mud. Father Michel was standing under the tree. His glasses were dotted with rain, and tiny beads of water were trapped in his short, tight curls. He smiled grimly. "Pascal. What are you doing out here in the rain?"

How to answer? "I'm waiting."

"For what? Your family?"

"Kind of. Yes. But they might be already here. I don't know."

Father Michel cocked one eyebrow as he thought. "I don't think I saw them arrive."

"How about my sister, Nadine? Did she come? Not very long ago?"

"Your sister? I don't . . . You can go inside and look for her if you like."

Hesitating, even though he wasn't really sure why. "I might wait out here a bit longer, if that's okay."

"If you're going to come all this way only to wait outside, why did you come at all?"

"I heard the bell," Pascal replied. "And I remembered what you said last week."

"What did I say?"

"That the church would be a safe place."

"And it is. Of course. After all, it's the house of God." Father Michel breathed out a heavy sigh as he glanced towards the church. "Well, when you're ready to come in, or if you want to check for your sister, you know you're welcome. But don't wait too long. The church is almost full."

Something else that didn't add up. He'd heard Father Michel telling people that there was plenty of room. But now he was saying that space was running out.

Watching Father Michel walking back to the church, his head bowed slightly against the rain. The bottom hem of his long white cassock was stained orange from the red mud.

And then, as Father Michel reached the front door and waved his hand to attract Father Oscar's attention, Pascal caught a glimpse of movement at the back of the church, down towards the seminary. A man who Pascal did not recognize as a priest had half-stepped out from behind the main classroom block. Then, just as quickly, he turned his head as if someone behind the building had spoken to him, and stepped quickly out of sight. But as he did so, he dropped something long, thin, metallic. It made a kind of jangling sound as it hit the rocky ground, and the man re-emerged briefly as he picked up the machete by its handle.

Tire marks led across the mud of the churchyard and behind the seminary. Pascal had never seen a car or truck of any kind drive through there. Father Michel didn't drive, and nor did any of the other priests, as far as he knew.

Tire marks. The man with the machete behind the classrooms. Perhaps more people back there with him, probably Jolts.

And all those people in the church. Perhaps one of those people was his sister.

And they were trapped.

He had to tell someone.

The trickle of people from the town had ceased, and Father Oscar had stopped ringing the bell. Pascal saw him release the thick rope. It swung gently, and Father Oscar placed his hand on it, stopped the swinging, ran his hand along it as if to put it to sleep. Then he turned and began to walk towards the church, his shoulders slumped.

Time to act. Pascal left his place behind the mango tree and ran towards Father Oscar, met him as he was halfway across the front churchyard.

"Father Oscar!"

Father Oscar looked up, flinched as he recognized Pascal. "Pascal! Why are you . . . ? What are you doing here?"

"There's Jolts down there," Pascal panted, pointing. "Behind the classrooms."

"Jolts?"

"Bad men. Men with machetes."

"Pascal, you shouldn't be here. Go home." Father Oscar tried to push past him, but Pascal stepped into his path. The priest stopped. Blinked. Surprised that a small boy would stand in his way.

"There's dead people down there," Pascal explained. "I can't go home. They killed Iggy."

"Who's Iggy?"

"Our goat. But I don't know why."

"I don't know either. Pascal, I'm telling you as a friend —"

"I don't even know where my parents are. Or my brother. Or my sister. Do you know where they are? Is Nadine in there, in the church?" So many questions that needed to be asked. So many questions that he'd held in for days now, just waiting to see someone he trusted so he could ask.

Father Oscar half-knelt as he placed his good hand on Pascal's shoulder. His voice was low. Barely more than a whisper. "Listen to me. I am telling you this *as a friend*. You have to get out of here. Now."

"Why?"

"Trust me, Pascal. Get out of here."

"But I don't know where —"

"Pascal, I haven't seen your parents, I haven't seen Jean-Baptiste, and I haven't seen Nadine. They're not here. Please believe me when I tell you, as a friend, that you must go, and you must go *now*. But you have to run. You have to run as if I'm trying to —"

"Where will I go?"

Staring deep into Pascal's eyes now. "You have to run as if I'm trying to stop you leaving, and you're running for your life."

"Why?"

"Because you are. I'll tell you to stop running. Don't listen to me."

Confused. "What . . . ?"

"When I grab your arm, you have to pull it away and run, do you hear me? Run into the jungle. I'll call out to you to stop. *Don't.* Don't stop. Do you understand?"

"Not really . . ."

"Do you understand what I'm asking you to do? I'll grab your arm, you'll yank it free and run, I'll tell you to stop, but you won't. You'll keep running. You won't look back. You'll stay out of sight, you'll find your sister and brother and parents, all right? But most important of all, you won't look back. Yes?" Father Oscar's eyes were brimming with tears. "Yes, Pascal?"

Pascal nodded.

"Good. Then do as I said, and do it now." He rested his hand on Pascal's forearm, and tightened his grip. His order was given in a whisper, but his command was as firm as if he'd shouted it. "*Now*, I said! *Go!*"

Tearing his arm free. Feeling nails scratching his skin as he pulled away and staggered backwards. Slipping in the mud, landing on his backside, feeling a slight twinge of satisfaction that he had been able to make it look so realistic.

"Pascal! Stop!"

Reminding himself to do the exact opposite. "No! Damn you!" It was more than the part required, and yet it felt good to say it. He could confess it later.

"Pascal! Get back here! The church is safe! I promise you!"

That last bit wasn't in the script. Stick to the part, he reminded himself. What they'd agreed.

"Go to hell!" he shouted over his shoulder.

Reaching the edge of the yard and the low, crooked fence. Throwing himself over it and rolling in the long, soaking grass.

He stopped, got to his knees and crawled back to the fence. He wasn't supposed to look back, but how could he not? He still wasn't sure why he'd had to pretend to run away in the first place.

Father Oscar was walking towards the church again. He reached Father Michel, who slipped an arm around him, said something close to his ear and patted him on the back. Father Oscar nodded and left in the opposite direction, towards the classroom block. And Father Michel reached inside his cassock and took out . . . a bunch of keys?

A bunch of keys.

And somewhere beyond the church, Pascal heard a truck start up.

Collège Secondaire de Saint Matthieu, Belgium

Friday 19 March 1999

Are you okay? Sir?

Yes. Thank you, Pascal. I'm fine.

You don't look fine.

So the trucks . . . The people behind the classrooms . . . The man with the . . .

Yes.

So am I right in assuming they came out from behind the buildings and went into the church?

Yes, they did, sir. Soldiers as well as other men with machetes and clubs and even shovels and hoes from the garden. They all went into the church. But not to pray.

Or to sing, I suppose.

Oh, they sang all right. But the songs they sang weren't hymns or anything like that. They were about killing the cockroaches, crushing them. No mercy, wipe out every last one. I remember the words well. At the time I thought it sounded like a TV advertisement for Jolt insect spray.

How many?

What?

How many people died?

In the church, or altogether? Maybe a thousand in the church, but it happened in lots of other churches as well. In our whole district, I think it was five or six thousand people.

And in all of Rwanda?

About eight hundred thousand.

In how long? A hundred days? That's ... that's almost eight thousand a day!

Yes. Eight thousand a day.

Pascal, did you ever find your sister?

Yes.

Alive?

Yes.

Your brother?

Yes.

Alive?

No.

Oh. I'm sorry. And your parents?

No.

So they died?

I know what happened to Papa.

Can you tell me?

They took him to Ruhengeri. They needed him to let them into the government garage where he worked. For the trucks.

And then they killed him?

That's what we think.

And your mother?

We don't really know.

So she might be alive, then?

It's possible. But I don't think so. It all happened five years ago, and there's been no sign of her. So we think... probably not.

I'm sorry. I have two more questions, Pascal. How did you escape? It seemed so ... hopeless.

I found my sister wandering down amongst the plantains. She still didn't know what was happening — not really. But she had found Macaron, so I guess that was something.

So, how did you get away?

A kind man who worked at the tourist lodge. He hid us in

the back of his truck and smuggled us over the border. That was pretty scary.

But then you were safe?

Not straight away. But eventually.

That sounds like quite a story.

It is. What was your second question?

Oh, yes. It's about the priests. How could they do such a thing?

Not all of them did. Lots of priests and nuns helped protect Tutsi people. People from other churches too. But the ones like Father Michel — do you know what they said when they were asked? "We are Hutu first, we are Catholic second."

That's . . . awful. Terrible. I'm so sorry, Pascal.

Sometimes I get very sad when I think about it. But at least some of my family are alive. Many people lost everyone.

That's true. So, Pascal, I need to ask you one final question, if I may. This whole process — talking to me about what happened — has it been useful?

For me?

Of course, for you. Have you found the whole experience useful?

For me, or for you?

I'm sorry, I don't understand. You were sent to talk to me. Why would *I* find it useful?

Well, does it make you feel better? Or worse?

Better or worse about what?

About what happened. Everyone in the world heard about what was happening in Rwanda, but they didn't do anything. Nothing. They just let it happen.

Does that make you angry?

What do you think? Would it make you angry?

I imagine it would.

Then yes, that's how I feel. Angry. And sad. Mostly sad.

Would you like to talk about it?

Maybe one day, I guess. But you probably wouldn't have time anyway.

I've plenty of time. Do *you* have time?

Me? I have all the time in the world.

ABOUT THE AUTHORS

James Roy is the author of over thirty books for children and young adults. Awards his books have won or been nominated for include the New South Wales Premier's Literary Award (Ethel Turner Prize), the Western Australian and Queensland premiers' book prizes, the Children's Book Council of Australia awards and the German Youth Literature Prize. He lives in the Blue Mountains just west of Sydney, and in his spare time he attempts to make music on a variety of instruments.

Noël Yandamutso Zihabamwe was born in 1983 in Butare, Southern Province, Rwanda, and spent much of his youth living as a refugee. Since moving to Australia he has gained degrees in the fields of social welfare, policy and development, and now works assisting migrants and refugees in their resettlement. Noël lives with his family in Liverpool, south-western Sydney, and spends his spare time organizing community and cultural events.

AUTHORS' NOTE

The plane carrying the president of Rwanda was shot down at 8:23 p.m. on Wednesday, April 6, 1994, just as most people were finishing the washing up from dinner. By the time of night that is darkest and coldest, the killing had already begun. And when the sun came up the next morning, the bodies of Rwandans were lying dead and dying in their houses, in their churches and in the streets.

One hundred days later, eight hundred thousand Rwandans were dead. Eight hundred thousand people in one hundred days. That's eight thousand a day. Every day. Today, tomorrow, the next day, the day after that, the day after that, over and over and over until you have counted to one hundred.

Why did it happen? In some ways it's relatively easy to explain, if you look at it with the eyes of a historian. But these weren't just numbers on a Wikipedia page — these were real people, with mothers and fathers and sons and daughters and brothers and sisters and neighbours and friends and classmates and teachers and homework and houses and pets and and and . . . and there were eight hundred thousand of them.

Why did we want to write this story, which was never going to be an easy one to tell? For James, it meant trying to get into the heads of people he'd never met, in a place he'd never been. It meant trying to imagine the fear and horror that was felt by the people who lived through the events of 1994, knowing all along that he could never even get close to knowing how that felt. And for Noël, it meant revisiting events he *did* live through, at the age of ten. These events took much of his family, and made him a refugee for the next ten years.

Most of all, we wanted to tell this story because we believe it's only by understanding the terrible and tragic events of the past that we can prevent similar events happening again in the future.

ACKNOWLEDGMENTS

I would like to thank my wife Vicki and the rest of my family for their patience, love and support, as ever; the University of New England, Armidale, New South Wales, where I was Writer in Residence in 2014; the May Gibbs Foundation, for granting me an Adelaide Fellowship in March 2014; the Rwandan and wider African community of Sydney for their warmth and generosity; Dyan Blacklock, for setting this train in motion, and for her patience; Celia Jellett, for her thoughtful edit and keen eye for detail; Phil Voysey and Cheryle Yin-Lo for making the initial connection; Noël, for sharing his story, and his beautiful wife Delphine and their family, for being so welcoming — much love to you all.

James Roy

I would like to thank and acknowledge my loving wife Delphine Marie Aimee Uwamwezi, for all her support, devotion and patience during the writing process; my late parents, Emmanuel and Judith Zihabamwe; my children, Kaylen and Jayden: I love you and the way you give me hope for other children around the world; James Roy, for all his support in realizing this book; my sisters, Brigitte Farrow and Anne Marie Zihabamwe and my nieces Enathe and Ariell, who supported me with encouragement, motivation and information. I also thank my brother-in-law Richard Farrow, who is a wonderful role model, as is Bertrand Tungandame, my elder brother in Sydney; Antoinette Uwera and her husband John, who are like my auntie and uncle in Sydney; my mother-in-law Christine Mukarugwiza for her courage and spiritual nurturing, and my late father-in-law for being a source of advice and moral leadership; both pairs of my "adopted" Australian parents, Sandra and Robert Lynch, and Maxine Chopard and Philip Pratley for their outstanding and continuing support. Without everyone mentioned above I would not be where I am now. Thank you.

Noël Zihabamwe